Book One in the Ties that Bind Series

Charisse

FAY
LAMB

Charisse

ISBN-13: 978-1-938092-42-8
ISBN-10: 1938092422

Published by Pix-N-Pens, 130 Prominence Point Pkwy. #130-330, Canton, GA 30114.

www.PixNPens.com

Printed in the United States of America.

Dedication

Charisse is a novel about grace, mercy and faith, but it's so much more to me than that. Friendships either weather the storms or fall apart, but true friendships carry with them memories of challenges, of laughter, and of tears.

Throughout my lifetime, I have made friendships with those who have made life's journey a better place for me:

Ronald Ray Johnson, we were together from birth until eight years old. Childhood promises we made to each other have shaped my life for the better. Wherever you are, please know that I have never ceased thinking of or praying for you.

Penny Blackwell Scott, you helped me weather my teenage years with your laughter and your acceptance. "Records breaking," is one of my all-time favorite memories.

Sandy Poore Wolfe, our friendship is cemented with laughter and tears—more of the former than the latter. I'm so glad you forgave me for "dropping" you out of the pool and for breaking your glasses and the myriad other crazy adventures we enjoyed.

Tracy Ruckman, my *youngest* friendship. We just click, don't we? And over the last year, your encouragement, faith in me, and your skill have been a blessing.

Marc Lamb, you are everything to me. My husband, my best friend, my confidant, my protector, and I pray every day that God will continue to fill our lives with love and with laughter. You are my Gideon. Go Gators!

Chapter One

The yellow finch perched on the birdfeeder outside Charisse Wellman's kitchen window did nothing for her mood. Beyond the songbird, her untended garden and yard that her husband, Vance, used to tend with great care reminded her why she hadn't slept.

Upstairs, a door creaked open. She waited for a moment, but her son didn't appear. "V.J., breakfast." She set the box of cereal on the table in her breakfast nook and returned to her window to stare out across the forlorn landscape. Like the weeds menacing the yard, irritation wound through every nerve in her body.

Lord, give me patience. He needs my love, not my anger.

Live up to your name, Charisse. That's what her husband would say. *You are grace, beauty, and kindness.*

She swiped the dishcloth over her countertop, past the marred Formica, and dipped it in the soapy dishwater. Her son's boundless vigor for anything other than dressing for school used to wring the energy from her in the same way she now twisted the dishrag to eliminate the water. One year was too long for either of them to endure this lack of vitality. Vance's death had zapped the life out of his wife and his child. She leaned both hands on the countertop and closed her eyes, expelling a worried exhale. Vance would know what to say to get their son hopping.

"V.J., we've got to hurry. You know I have an appointment."

"Okay." Her seven-year-old bounded down the stairs. A seldom-seen smile pushed his lips upward. "I'm ready. I can't wait to see the shuttle. Timmy told me there are alligators in big ditches on the side of the road. He said the shuttle's cool, and you can see a real live astronaut suit." He pulled out his chair and plopped down.

"Mommy grew up in Titusville. Remember?" They could see the Vehicle Assembly Building and the launch pads across the river from her mother's house. You'd think he'd never seen a shuttle launch. He'd viewed plenty before they shut down the program.

His smile vanished. Her careless words had dampened his enthusiasm.

Charisse winced. Neither a trace of kindness nor an ounce of grace remained. She was sure if there had ever been any beauty on either the outside or the inside, it had faded away in the last year.

She'd just tossed a precious gift away. V.J. smiled so rarely these days.

Why hadn't she thought of taking a day trip to the space center? Yeah, she'd grown up with it, took the whole space exploration thing for granted, but who knew the adventure would make such a difference in him? She put a smile in place. "Oh, honey, I know you're excited. Field trips are so much fun."

He'd begged her not to go on the job interview, to join him on the class outing, but he'd accepted her answer

the way he braved most disappointments these days—
with sad eyes and a silent mouth.

Charisse poured the cereal and then the milk into the
bowl as the toaster presented its specialty—burnt bread.

The phone rang, and V.J. jumped up. "I got it." He
grabbed for it.

She took the phone from him. "Sit down and finish
your breakfast so I can drop you at school before my
appointment." She brushed back an unruly strand of
blonde hair.

"Good morning," a familiar voice greeted.

"Libby." Remembering a promise she'd broken to
her friend, Charisse made a face in her son's direction and
received an uncharacteristic giggle in reward. "I'm sorry I
didn't call you last night to let you know we made it
home. No more late Sunday evening meetings. By the
time I picked V.J. up from my mom's, drove back to
Orlando, got him into bed, and ironed my clothes for this
morning, well—I'm exhausted."

And she'd used her last bit of coffee yesterday, trying
to get herself ready and awake for church. Until she could
add that luxury back onto her grocery list, she'd have to
suffer through her mornings without caffeine. If she
stepped down from the high school reunion committee,
she could use the gas savings to purchase her daily energy
boost.

"That's okay. I didn't call to make you feel guilty. I
only wanted to check on you." Libby's sweet voice
calmed Charisse.

Coffee or no coffee, how could she think of quitting
the reunion committee no matter the cost? The only

reason she'd taken on the duty was to support Libby and give her friend a chance to get out of the house—a much needed break from her wonderful, but ailing, mother.

"Mommy, can I have some extra money to buy you a present from the gift shop? Timmy says they have a good one."

"Are you okay?" Libby asked.

"Yes," Charisse answered both their questions.

She looked at the jar filled with the change Vance used to empty from his pockets each evening. Today, to keep the smile on her little boy's face, she'd do the unthinkable.

V.J. smiled and went back to his breakfast. "I'll buy you some astronaut ice cream. Timmy says it's not even cold." Milk dribbled down his chin.

"I'm fine," she said to Libby and moved to the jar, pulling out quarters and reminding herself that whatever V.J. bought would be a special gift from his father as well.

Libby chattered on, but Charisse wasn't listening.

She counted the quarters until she had enough and stacked them beside the long deep scratch on her Formica countertop. As if cleaning fish inside the house hadn't been enough, Vance had marred her perfect kitchen with his fillet knife. She'd exploded with anger at him.

"I'm sorry," he'd said. "Sweetheart, I didn't mean to cut into the counter. I'll replace it. I promise." He tilted his head waiting for her to forgive him. His brown-eyed look resembled a chastised puppy.

"You bet you will," she'd said before storming away.

Charisse gripped the phone in her hand and ran her hand along the scratch then placed her forefinger and thumb at the bridge of her nose attempting to stop her emotions. She'd meant to apologize the next day before he left for work, but pandemonium had broken loose when her car wouldn't start. Then after work when he'd picked her up from her class at the university, she'd never gotten the chance.

His ready apology and the forgiveness she failed to speak remained forever etched into her heart. She'd never allow anyone to change the countertop—a reminder to her that some things weren't all that important after all.

"… besides, you seemed preoccupied at the reunion meeting." Libby's words brought her back, and she froze. What had she been talking about?

"Do you need my help with anything on our agenda?" Libby asked. "I could call the country club and do some of the legwork."

"No. I can handle it. Thank you, though. I'll call today and make an appointment with the manager before our next committee meeting. I'll get everything done in one visit. You have enough to worry about, Lib."

"Do you want to talk?"

"I'm fine," Charisse said again, but the quiver in her voice betrayed her. The tower of strength she'd built day by day since Vance's death threatened to crumble.

"You don't sound it. Tell me, and I'll pray for you."

She stared at the coins in her hand. Libby, sweet Libby. Prayer came so natural to her friend.

"I told you I might have to drop out of law school," she whispered. "The money's not there, not enough for me to go to school and keep the house. The insurance pays the mortgage. That's all. I'm not going back."

"Oh, Charisse. I'm sorry. I know how much it means to you. Why didn't you say something last night? We could have talked and prayed together."

And that's why she hadn't mentioned it. She hated to put her failure into words. When she started law school, Vance made her promise she'd finish no matter what. Did he realize "no matter what" would turn out to be his death?

Scattering the coins, she covered her eyes with her hand. Still, the tears seeped through. "I need to find a job. I have an interview today, but my faith is lacking."

"You're not going to forget school completely, are you?"

"I could continue if V.J. and I want to live in my car." The words she'd meant to convey humor only added to the pain crushing her heart.

Life wasn't fair. Vance should be alive. She should be in school. V.J. should be happy and well adjusted. At the very least, her husband's killer should be in jail. Instead, her old high school friend, the Honorable Gideon Tabor, had entered a directed verdict, taking the decision from the jury and making it himself, and he'd dismissed the charges following the state's presentation of its case.

What was Gideon thinking? She hadn't seen him in years, and as a witness, she wasn't allowed in the courtroom. He didn't know the defendant, Carson Fullwell, had killed her husband. Not that it would matter. Gideon had dismissed her from his life long ago. His mocking words still haunted her.

Charisse dropped the hand covering her eyes and leaned her head back. *What if the interview I have today is with ...?* No. God wouldn't put her in that position. What would she do if the interview ended up being with Gideon?

"What's wrong, Mommy?" V.J. tugged at her skirt. "Don't cry."

Charisse bent down and held her son close, nearly dropping the phone. "Mommy's having a rough morning. Are you finished eating?"

She felt his nod against her shoulder, and she knew. She'd do anything she had to do to keep her son in the only home he'd ever known, even if it meant working for the man who allowed Vance's killer to go free.

"Mommy," V.J. pulled away from her, "is it because you can't go on the trip with me? It's okay."

She forced a smile and kissed his cheek. "Thank you for telling me so. I would really like to go, but you know my appointment is very important. Now, why don't you go get your books?"

"I don't need them. The field trip, remember?"

"Mommy's being silly." She forced a lighter tone. "Of course you don't need your books." V.J. needed security and her runaway emotions would provide only instability. "You know how Libby is. She always makes Mommy cry." She pulled away and winked at him.

"Charisse, I'd never make you cry on purpose." A very patient and quiet Libby missed the joke, as only Libby would do.

"Hi, Libby." V.J. took the phone from Charisse's hand. "I'm going to Kennedy Space Center today to see the big rocket ships, and I'm going to buy Mommy some ice cream like the astronauts eat."

Charisse packed his lunch as her son rambled on. When she finished, she took the phone and pointed toward the stairs. "Go brush your teeth."

"I haven't heard him talk so much since …" Libby stopped.

"Since Vance died. I know. The Lord is giving me a little encouragement this morning." Charisse washed and rinsed the cereal bowl, leaving it in the dish rack.

"Don't give up on your dreams, not until you're sure God doesn't have another plan in the works for you."

"I thought God wanted Vance in my life." Bitterness seeped into her words.

"That man was pure blessing."

"And God took him away. I can tell V.J. how wonderful his father was, but he'll never experience Vance's love again. His father will become a distant memory." Charisse sighed. "A stranger ran my husband down and left the scene. My last memory of Vance is his broken and bloodied body on the side of that road, and Gideon Tabor used some loophole to release his killer.

"I mean, I've been to law school. Directed verdicts aren't easy to win. The state attorney had to have been a blithering idiot to take a case to trial if there was a chance the verdict would be taken out of the jury's hands and delivered by the judge before the defense even began its case. If the state had called me, I might have been able to convince Gideon."

"Of what? How many times have you told me you didn't get a good look at the car or the driver, only Vance?"

Charisse choked back the sob brought forth by Libby's steadfast truth. "But it was Fullwell's car. The other witnesses confirmed the tag number. The car was registered to the man."

"Charisse, I know it's hard to let go, but God's given you another direction. Please trust Him to lead you."

"I'm trying." Charisse looked at the clock on the kitchen wall. She straightened. "I have to hurry. V.J. has to get to school by eight thirty, and my interview is at nine. In rush hour traffic, I'm pushing it." And she had to stop by a convenience store and change the quarters into bills for V.J. to carry with him on his field trip. "Pray for me, please."

"You know I will. Godspeed."

"Love you." Charisse clicked off the phone. "V.J., let's go."

The door to his chambers opened, but Gideon Tabor didn't look up from the résumé in his hand. Only two people entered his office without knocking. He enjoyed the visits of one and dreaded the company of the other.

"So, how's life treatin' you this Monday morning, young Judge Gideon?" This visitor he enjoyed. Judge Deacon Foster tugged at his blue bow tie and stretched his neck as if trying to get free from a noose.

Gideon lifted his own tie—a little worn, but it held a special place in his heart. He used to call it his lucky tie. This morning, he needed all the help he could get. Good thing he'd prayed regarding today's interviews. God's provision had replaced the luck in his tie some months ago.

"Whatcha got?" Deacon sat in the chair in front of Gideon's desk.

Gideon held out the résumé, his eyes lingering on the woman's name. He'd give anything for it to be her. He shook the thought from his head. There were many women in the world named Charisse. He released the résumé to his friend and mentor. "How'd you find the perfect law clerk?"

Deacon rubbed the gray stubble on his chin. "I guess I knew Zelma was the right one for me when she answered the most important question without blinkin' an eye."

"And what question did you ask?"

"A clerk is like a wife. You have to have one who's compatible so that sooner or later she begins readin' your mind and knows what you need before you need it."

"So?"

"I asked her where her favorite fishin' hole's located. I asked everyone I interviewed the same question, and she's the only one who answered right from the get-go."

"What'd she say?"

"She said," Deacon raised his southern twang two octaves, "'I'm not here to discuss fishin' holes, Judge Foster. I'm here to interview for a job. You hire me, and

I'll tell you where you can find the best fishin' in all of Florida.'"

"And?" Gideon lifted a brow.

"Haulover Canal on the Space Coast."

"I know where it is," Gideon lifted a brow. "I'm from Titusville, remember?"

Deacon held the résumé at arm's length and narrowed his eyes. The old man was forever losing his reading glasses. "Charisse Wellman's very impressive on paper." He handed it back.

Gideon looked over the woman's credentials once again. "Second year law student. I wonder why she isn't asking for an internship rather than a job."

Deacon shrugged. "Many of 'em find out they can't hack it in this profession. Research is one thing. Court appearances are another."

Gideon shook his head. He didn't buy Deacon's line of logic. "I don't get the same feeling from this one. She's got a lot going for her—maybe too much. Something's not right."

"Gid, you've interviewed twenty hopefuls since Stacey left. Who are you lookin' to find, Della Street?"

Gideon laughed. "Actually, I'm trying to find someone Delilah James won't scare off. Della Street might be the perfect candidate."

"How are you and the Right Honorable Delilah these days?"

"As long as we stay away from the subject of God and limit our sparring matches to five minutes, we survive each round."

"You don't recognize a golden opportunity when you see one, do you? Keep talkin' about God. It's like garlic to that she-wolf."

"You're confusing your horror tales." Gideon shook his head.

"Just take the advantage the Lord has given you, and use it to get her out of your personal life," Deacon advised.

"I want to set a good example for her. Pulling away isn't the answer."

"Just remember even Jesus told his disciples to shake the sand off their feet when His precious gift wasn't well received." Deacon pushed himself up from the chair and walked out the door. Then he leaned back in. "And hire someone today. Delilah's less than adequate clerk is complainin', and Zelma would rather work for you than for me."

"Thanks. I appreciate the pressure."

Deacon studied him for a moment. "Another thing to consider when you're hirin' is whether the person you take on will watch your back." He smiled and shook a crooked finger at Gideon. "My Zelma's a bulldog. Hire someone like her, and you'll do fine."

Gideon stared at the name on the paper in front of him. Charisse Wellman. Her résumé was too full of college accolades to leave much room for personal information. Was she married, divorced, never married, a widow? No, too young for a widow. Her college years lined up with his. She was his age. The same age as Charisse Taylor.

Gideon turned his chair, leaned back, and stared at
the Orlando skyline from his office window. He smiled at
the memory playing across his mind. Charisse Taylor. Her
name was beautiful. *She* was beautiful.

The guys on his high school football team used to
tease him about his crush on her. They said she was fat,
didn't wear the right clothes, and was too shy and nerdy.

"You don't have a clue," he'd told them. Charisse
Taylor was perfect. Thick blonde hair fell straight to her
waist. Sweet round face. Blue eyes the color of a summer
sky that always looked at him as if he could do no wrong.

The picture in his mind faded and his smile vanished.
He'd hurt her feelings, and he'd never gotten the chance
to apologize. Lately, he was overwhelmed with the desire
to see her again, to let her know her friendship and her
words of concern for him had made a difference in his
life. Now, because of her, he wanted to help others.

He lost track of her after high school—not that she'd
ever want to see him again. Especially after the way he'd
treated her. The ugly scene still churned his gut after all
this time, but he allowed the pain to wash over him,
allowed another replay of the last time he'd spoken with
her.

Gideon and his mother had buried his father that day,
two weeks before graduation, but his grief couldn't justify
what he'd done. When Charisse tried to comfort him,
tried to tell him about her belief in God and how the Lord
had helped her to survive the grief she'd suffered over her
father's abandonment, he'd laughed at her—a nasty
chortle filled with rage. He'd lashed out, calling her
stupid and naïve. "My father's dead. Don't you get it? My

father didn't want to leave. Dad loved me. You can pretend God is your father. He's not mine. God took mine away."

Those big, gorgeous eyes of hers, already filled with hurt for his pain, had flooded with tears. Big crystal drops spilled down her cheeks.

Gideon dashed a hand across his eyes to clear the memory of her face. How many times had he called himself a fool for devastating his sweet, innocent friend? In one terrible moment, he'd destroyed the only friendship that meant anything. Dumb kid that he was, he hadn't known how to apologize.

He turned back to his desk and picked up the résumé. No woman named Charisse could live up to his memories, but all he needed to know about Charisse Wellman were her credentials and her abilities to do the research he'd need. And Deacon was right. He needed someone who'd watch his back and keep him out of trouble when it came to the manipulative Judge Delilah James.

Charisse paused in front of the emblem of the Ninth Judicial Circuit and peered through the glass entry at the receptionist. Taking a deep breath to steady her nerves, she pushed open the door and walked toward the desk in the center of the room. The woman held up one finger as she spoke into the phone.

Charisse stared down the long hall beyond the woman. Offices with glass windows lined the right side.

On the left gold plates identified the judges who worked inside the windowless rooms.

The Honorable Deacon Foster.

The Honorable Delilah James.

Charisse smiled. A Deacon and a Delilah. What would be the name of the next judge? Usher? Pew? Samson?

Gideon?

She'd known the possibility existed. Her smile vanished. *Really, Lord? You wouldn't. Would You?*

She dug through her purse and brought out her glasses. She'd need them for her interview. She slipped them on and peered at the door further down the hall and grimaced.

The Honorable Gideon Tabor.

The receptionist put down her phone. "May I help you, ma'am?" Her southern accent spilled over with her friendly smile—not a Floridian, a Georgia peach.

Maybe the interview was with another judge. The court administrator's office hadn't specified who needed a clerk. "I'm here to interview for the law clerk position."

"That'll be with Judge Tabor. You have a seat. I'll let him know you're here."

Charisse nodded and moved toward one of the chairs against the wall.

She gulped down the emotions playing tug of war with her insides. *Run.* She started to turn away.

She stopped. The electric bill was past due.

But she couldn't work for Gideon Tabor, not after he let Vance's killer go free. She closed her eyes.

She could live without a lot of things, but electricity kept the meager food in the refrigerator from spoiling. It provided warm water for V.J.'s baths.

She brought a fisted hand against her leg. *Vance, I need you.*

But Vance was gone, and she was here—alone. She needed to provide for her son—even if she had to push down her anger every day and keep her hands from strangling the big dope who might hire her.

Gideon Tabor, quarterback extraordinaire, the hero of innumerable girls attending Astronaut High School. Wasn't everyone excited about his attendance at the reunion and his induction into the Astronaut High School Athletic Hall of Fame? She was probably the only one who didn't look forward to seeing him.

She could have forgiven him for making her feel small and stupid during high school the night she tried to comfort him, but she could never absolve him for taking away the closure she and her son needed for Vance's death.

She looked toward the exit. If she left, she could avoid seeing Gideon.

No. She'd given up a field trip with her son. If she walked out now, she'd miss a job opportunity and make V.J.'s sacrifice worthless. And if they were going to die of heat exhaustion in the sweltering Florida temps, unable to run their air conditioning without electricity, or from starvation, she'd rather know she'd done everything she could to prevent it.

Gideon Tabor or no Gideon Tabor she had to find work.

She sat, straight as a board, and brought her fingers to her mouth, stopping short of chewing her nails. She placed her hands in her lap and pressed them into tight fists, one enfolding the other.

For goodness' sake, he was only a man—a man who'd made a terrible mistake.

Sooner or later she'd expected to run into him. After all, he would most likely attend the reunion. Truth was, though, Charisse thought about not attending. She'd help prepare and simply not show for the event.

She shook the thought from her mind. That was the old Charisse talking. She hadn't run from a challenge in years. But could she face Gideon and remain civil after what he'd done? Well, she'd get the chance to find out shortly—if she decided to stay.

She looked toward the exit then glanced at her watch. Much longer and she'd bolt.

"Ma'am, are you okay?" Georgia Peach asked. "Judge Tabor, he's a nice fella. You don't have to be nervous."

Charisse nodded, her smile stiff. "Thank you." She brushed her ever-annoying hair from her face and pulled at a strand. All through high school she'd colored and even curled her hair. Now, she had no time or money for such luxuries. What you saw was what you got—a shade darker and straight as the invisible arrow she'd like to put in Gideon Tabor's heart.

"Ms. Wellman?"

Charisse sprang to her feet at the sound of the all-too familiar voice. She dropped her purse and leaned down to pick it up. Her glasses slid off her face. She picked them up, too.

Standing, she slipped the glasses on and straightened her skirt. Again, she brushed the strands from her face. One strand caught in the bend of her glasses, and she winced.

After all these years, she found herself looking up into rich jade eyes. His thick brown hair was cut short, a few wayward strands hanging over the right side of his forehead. What she would have given to see a middle-age paunch, but Gideon didn't have an ounce of fat on him that she could see. He looked as trim and athletic as ever. Time had only enhanced his good looks.

A slow smile pushed his familiar dimples into place. He tilted his head. Because she'd long ago memorized his every gesture, Charisse waited for his acknowledgement.

"Charisse Taylor? You've got to be kidding me. It's good to see you. How have you been?"

Her disloyal heart played her ribcage like a xylophone. She shook the traitorous thoughts away and focused on the exit. "You know, Gideon, I think this was a bad idea. I need to leave." With a deep breath, Charisse hurried toward the door.

"Charisse, wait."

She turned.

He lopped after her like an eager puppy.

With her hand on the door, she pushed it open a bit. A vision of V.J. eating yet another peanut butter and jelly sandwich for dinner stopped her from moving any further, but she couldn't look into the face the big buffoon.

"Gideon, I'm sorry for wasting your time, but I—I'm sure I'm not the person for this job."

"Why don't you let me make that decision?"

She'd allowed him to crush her heart twice now. Could she chance a third pummeling?

Her mobile phone rang, and she snatched it from her purse, mindful that V.J. was on a field trip and accidents could always happen. Her shoulders slumped at the number. The bank, calling about her overdue car payment. Could things get any worse? She stuffed the phone into her purse and turned, still, not meeting his eyes.

"Come on. Let's talk," Gideon coaxed.

The phone dinged, indicating the bank representative had left a voice mail message. That gave her two choices. She could walk out of the office and never see Gideon Tabor again, and soon—very soon—they'd come for her car, the repo guy probably finding her and V.J. sitting in a house without electricity, no food in the refrigerator, and a foreclosure note on her front door.

Her other choice was just a little more inviting.

Charisse nodded and followed Gideon.

"Judge Tabor, Attorney John Turner's calling for you." The receptionist held up her receiver.

"Thank you, Marlene. Come on in, Charisse." Gideon motioned her into his office and shut the door behind them. "This is a very important call. Have a seat, and I'll be right with you."

Charisse sat, took a deep breath, and let it out slowly. *Lord, protect my tongue. Let me get out of here without the humiliation of telling him exactly what I think of him.*

I'll apply for a job at the burger joint on Orange Blossom Trail and be happy with it.

"John, are we on for the game tonight?" Gideon offered her a sheepish grin at his obvious joke about the importance of the call.

His little boy mannerisms caused her breath to catch. He hadn't changed.

And down deep, past the pain and anger, neither had she.

Her gaze flitted to the diplomas hanging on tan walls. Their mahogany frames matched the wood of his desk, the credenza behind him, and the two bookshelves to his right. Gideon had graduated from the University of Florida with a Bachelor of Arts. He'd also been accepted into and graduated from UF's law school.

Impressive.

Especially since he'd needed her help in every one of his high school courses. Always a data source. Never a date.

"Okay, I'll see you around seven. You can buy the snacks. Yeah, I know. I got the better bargain."

Gideon put the phone down and leaned forward. "How have you been?"

"I'm fine, Judge Tabor, and you?"

"Gideon, Charisse. We're old friends."

She bit down on her tongue and pushed aside her emotions. Yes, they'd once been friends. Now, though, Charisse stood on the battlefield of grief alone, and her clueless enemy had no idea of the anger she fought to contain.

Gideon picked up a paper in front of him—her résumé. She'd dropped it off at the court administrator's office the week before.

"You look remarkable on paper. Valedictorian. I remember how excited you were when you were accepted into Tulane. I see you returned to Florida—Stetson Law School." He looked up at her as if he expected her to say something.

Charisse bit down harder.

"You participated in moot court. Tell me a little about it."

She straightened and smoothed her skirt. She could do this. "I was a finalist in the moot court competition in my first year of law school. I declined acceptance on the team in my second year when I made the *Law Review*."

Gideon leaned forward. Mention of the publication of her research would peak his interest.

"My paper concerned the laws governing grandparental custody, or the significant absence of same without evidence of abuse, abandonment, or the death of the parents."

He glanced once more at her application. "This community service you performed, what did you do?"

"I worked with a retired judge in Volusia County. He developed a program to teach elementary school children in underprivileged areas about the law." No need to tell him she'd actually written the curriculum. "We went into classrooms throughout Central Florida and presented them with an overall view of criminal law, civil law, torts, and the responsibility of all individuals in the legal system. Judge Kenley is still gathering the statistics on the program to determine if teaching children about the law is a deterrent to crime."

He studied her résumé. Then he studied her. "Are you familiar with Westlaw software?"

"Very much so. During my second year of law school, I taught the program to first year students." Charisse moved up and sat on the edge of her seat.

"Okay, say I need the latest ruling by the Fifth District Court of Appeals on the admissibility of a Breathalyzer following a traffic stop for DUI, officer has probable cause due to civil infraction; defendant passes all other sobriety tests. Show me how you'd locate it, and print me out a copy."

He stood and motioned Charisse to take his seat. She moved around his desk, and he held the chair out for her. She sank into the luxurious leather and felt the warmth left by his body. Her hands trembled. She willed them to be still as she moved the mouse to the menu. She clicked on the correct database within the program. Within seconds she found the information he needed and printed out the results.

Leaning close to her, he pulled the papers from his printer and moved to the other side of his desk to sit in her seat, indicating she should remain in his. She let a smile play across her lips. Gideon was always comfortable. Nothing took him off guard—except the death of his father.

"Impressive on paper and in person. Do you have plans to finish law school?"

Charisse glanced over his shoulder for a brief second, stilling the disappointment that threatened to bubble to the surface. She cleared her throat. "No, not in the near future." She waited another second to further gain control. "I do plan to continue someday."

"What's stopping you now?"

Charisse looked down and picked at the seam on the leather chair. Then she lifted her chin, meeting his gaze. "Finances." She forced the word out. "I'm sorry. This is hard to talk about." So much for her attempted bravado. She took a deep breath and quieted her trembling lips.

"I can imagine your husband probably hates that you have to quit school."

Charisse pinched her lips together for a long moment and tried to remember that although Gideon had let Vance's killer go free, he had not taken Vance away from her. Someone else had—someone Gideon allowed to get away with murder. "My husband died a little more than a year ago. It's just my boy and me now."

An unreadable look flitted across Gideon's face. Pity, most likely.

Charisse steeled against it.

"I'm very sorry, Charisse. How old is your boy?"

A bright light and a turn in the conversation. She snatched at the distraction and smiled. "V.J. just turned seven."

"V.J.?"

"He's named after his father."

Gideon continued to watch her for a long moment.

Charisse fought to keep eye contact with him while refusing to offer any other information.

He stood. "Have you heard about our upcoming class reunion?"

"I'm on the committee." She left the comfort of his chair, hoping the interview was over and readying for a quick escape.

"Giddy." The door slammed open. "Oh." The raven-haired beauty stopped and looked from Gideon to Charisse who still stood behind Gideon's desk.

The woman placed her hands on the curve of her hips, her long manicured nails tapping on her too tight skirt, her brown eyes narrowing like a cat ready to fight for its favorite toy. "And who is this?" She moved close to Gideon, flipping up his tie. "You know I hate this tired old rag."

His father had given him that tie before his induction into the National Honor Society. The memory jumped out at Charisse, startling her. Had she really been so infatuated with him that she remembered a gift he'd received from his dad? Worse yet, she still remembered his birthday and his favorite food.

So much for despising the very ground he walked upon.

"Charisse Tay—I'm sorry." Gideon looked down at her résumé on his desk. "Charisse Wellman, I'd like you to meet Judge Delilah James. Dee, we're in the middle of something here."

"Let's have lunch." The judge straightened the tie she'd messed up, her hand lingering against Gideon's chest for longer than Charisse thought appropriate, but who was she to say?

"Give me a minute to speak with Ms. Wellman, and we'll discuss it." Gideon stepped away from her touch.

Delilah didn't leave.

Gideon's mouth parted, and he breathed in, releasing it with a sudden rush—a sign of great annoyance. Another thing she remembered about him.

Charisse moved around the desk and bent to pick up her purse she'd left by the chair. This time, she caught her glasses before they slid completely off her nose. She tossed them into the handbag.

When she straightened, Gideon held out his hand. "Charisse, can I reach you at the number on your résumé?"

She nodded and slipped her hand into his warm, strong grasp.

"Oh, Giddy, it's just an interview. Let her go. Let's do lunch."

Gideon took another deep breath, but he didn't release Charisse from his gaze or his hold. "Does your son enjoy basketball?"

"Basketball, baseball, any sport. He used to spend all his time outside playing with his father—"

"Oh, really, Gid. Does anyone care about this?" The other woman lifted her eyes to the ceiling and shook her head.

If V.J. acted that way, Charisse would send him to his room.

Charisse gave a tiny shake of her head at the woman's rudeness and then met Gideon's steadfast gaze again. "Thank you for your time, Judge Tabor." She pulled her hand free and started for the door.

"Ms. Wellman?"

She turned at the hint of amusement in his voice.

"Charisse. One more question. Could you recommend a church?"

"Gideon Tabor, you can't ask that question," Judge James scolded like a pouting dark-haired Barbie.

Charisse ignored the woman. "I'm sure you can find several in whatever denomination you want right in your area. An Internet search would be helpful."

"I'm looking for a church home, not just a place to attend on Sunday mornings. Where do you go?"

Charisse bit the inside of her cheek for a long second. Hadn't she always wanted Gideon to know the love of Christ? And he seemed so sincere. She let her shoulders drop, tension easing away. "I attend a small church, Calvary Fellowship. We'd love to have you visit."

"I just might. I'm a fairly new Christian, and I do need a church family."

Charisse tried to stop the smile, but it sprang out of nowhere. God had spread balm over one of her wounds.

"She could sue the pants off this county for that question." Judge James's whine threatened to pull the scab right off.

If Charisse hadn't sent a barrage of complaints to the court administrator for what Gideon had done to her and her son, she wasn't about to start litigation over such a harmless question that so clearly showed God had heard Charisse's prayers for Gideon petitioned so long ago.

"It's not part of the interview. It has nothing to do with whether I hire her or not. I took the liberty because Charisse and I are old friends. I'm sorry if I offended you, Charisse."

"You could never offend me by asking a question about my church," Charisse assured him and looked to the woman. "Judge James, the Orange County legal system is in no danger of a lawsuit from me whether or not I'm hired. Judge Tabor's question will be our little secret, and should anyone ask me about it, I'll deny it as nothing but friendly chatter between two people with a similar love for God."

Judge James smirked. "Well, aren't you a little bulldog?"

When Charisse turned back to Gideon, he pulled his elbow past his side with his fist clenched upward—his favorite sign for victory. Something he used to do when his receivers or running backs scored a touchdown or when he finally got his head wrapped around a mathematical problem.

She smiled at his antics, and his face reddened. She held out her hand once again. "Judge Tabor, it has been so nice to see you."

She wished her words were a lie, but she meant them. And that made her angry.

Chapter Two

Gideon waited in the aisle of the Amway Center as John Turner made his way through the people crouching in their seats to allow him passage. Then, excusing himself, he did the same, sitting in the seat beside his friend and former law partner.

"Charisse is amazing. I phoned each of her references and talked to a professor I know at Stetson," Gideon continued the conversation they'd begun outside. "The only fault I can find with her is she's too humble. She said she worked for this judge on a study. The guy tells me she wrote the materials he used. No other applicant comes close to her credentials."

John whistled at a vendor hawking nachos. He dug in his pocket and passed money down the aisle. In return, the vendor passed the food to him. "So, hire her. What's the problem?"

"Remember the girl I told you about, Charisse Taylor?"

John studied him. "Maybe you shouldn't hire her, Gid. Your choice depends on whether you want to ask her out or have a competent law clerk."

"She looks and acts differently than she did when we were younger." She'd lost a lot of weight, but heavy or thin, she was beautiful.

But it was in her poise. Until the end of the interview, he'd felt like he faced an old enemy instead of the girl he admired in high school, the one whose attention he'd worked so hard to gain.

The smile she'd given him at his blatant hint that he'd finally gotten the Message she'd tried to share with him so long ago, that was pure gold to him.

"So are you going to hire your old girlfriend or not? Seems to me a clerk with her credentials could find a job with no problem at all. If you're not going to offer her the position, send her my way." John dipped his nacho into the cheese, ate half of it, and slipped the remaining portion back into the melted mixture.

"Unfortunately, she was never my girlfriend. I was a dolt. Charisse Wellman is a different person than the girl I knew as Charisse Taylor. She's more self-assured. You should have seen the way she handled your favorite judge."

"Delilah?"

"Oh, yeah. The younger Charisse would have wilted under Delilah's non-existent charm. For a moment, I got the idea she'd take on Delilah if she posed a threat to me."

"Really?" John held out the nachos.

"You double-dipped." Gideon waved them off. "I'd rather eat after my dog."

John laughed. "Tell me more about this woman who would dare oppose the intimidating force known as Delilah."

"She spoke back." Gideon shrugged. "No one does that to Dee. Well, Deacon, but it's just an enjoyable pastime for him."

"And the younger Charisse wouldn't?"

"No. The girl I knew was sweet, and I loved everything about her—including her insecurities and her shyness. Charisse Wellman is a strong woman. I saw some vulnerability when she mentioned her son and deceased husband, but otherwise, she's really self-assured."

The big burly guy who owned the seats in front of Gideon's nodded a hello as he made his way along his aisle. Gideon had never carried on a conversation with the bearded fellow who wore his blue and black jersey with pride, but during each game, they high-fived each other over good plays.

The main lights dimmed, and spotlights bounced across the court. People stood to cheer as the announcer introduced the Orlando Magic players.

"Do you know what I think?" John leaned toward him, yelling above the crowd.

Gideon waited.

"Hire her. If she stood up against Delilah during an interview, what will she do if she works for you? You said she's qualified. No brainer, buddy."

Gideon nodded. He'd already prayed about the decision. Deacon had all but ordered him to give Charisse Wellman a chance, and John had confirmed it for him.

Charisse opened the stack of bills and placed them into their return envelopes. She wrote the due dates in the corner where a stamp would cover the writing—if she ever managed to get the money to pay them. She'd already canceled the cable and the newspaper. Her contract with her cellular company ended last month, and her mobile phone was the next luxury to go. She made every meal stretch for two or three days, if possible. Hand-me-downs from a family at church were the only reason V.J. wasn't wearing clothes he had all but outgrown.

There wasn't much else they could live without. If she didn't find a job soon, her little boy would lose the last bit of stability she'd been able to keep for him—the only home he'd ever known. The allotment she'd set up from the proceeds of Vance's life insurance paid out only enough for the mortgage. What good was a beautiful home if you had no electricity, water, or food?

The phone rang, and Charisse closed her eyes. "Dear God, thank You for the payment of the mortgage and the roof over our head and for the food that nourishes us. I don't mean to take Your gifts lightly. Lord, I don't know how to do this. My faith is wavering under this mountain of responsibility. Please show me how to dig out from under it one shovelful at a time."

The phone continued to ring.

"V.J., answer the phone, please." She rubbed tired eyes.

Where was the son the Lord had given her this morning? V.J. had returned to his stoicism as soon as he slumped into the car after school. With the field trip over, he seemed to have no real expectation of another exciting adventure, and with her lack of funds, what could she offer?

After another ring, she heard his soft answer. Several seconds passed while she placed the bills in the order they were due.

"Mommy?" V.J. walked into the dining room.

"Yes, baby."

He held out the phone. "He says he's Judge Tabor."

At the sound of the name, Charisse's heart lurched. Was this God's answer to prayer or would He test her faith even further? What was she thinking? Working with Gideon Tabor would stretch her faith to the max.

Charisse took the phone, covering it with her hand. "You need to take a bath. Is your homework ready for me to look over?"

V.J. nodded.

"I love you." She blew him a kiss.

"Love you, too." He turned and plodded up the steps.

"Hello," she said.

A loud cheering crowd answered back.

"Yeah, that's the way. Rebound!"

Charisse pulled the phone from her ear at Gideon's enthusiastic roar. She held it away from her until the cheers died down. Then she waited.

"Charisse?"

"Yes." She couldn't stop the picture his enthusiasm brought back to her. He'd once cheered her on in a math competition in much the same way, and the organizers were none too happy with his jock-like mentality where academics were concerned.

"I'm sorry." Without seeing his face, she recognized the smile in his words, which were spoken loudly over the rumbling crowd in the background.

"Quite all right." She studied the pile of bills while she raised her voice so he could hear.

There would be more in the mail tomorrow, and the next day, and the next.

"Have you taken another position?"

Oh, no. Was God handing her that shovel she'd mentioned in her prayer? "No, I haven't." Charisse closed her eyes. *Whatever you want, Lord. Whatever you have for me—Gideon or the burger place. I'll follow.*

"Well, I assume I'm still in the running," he spoke over the noise.

"I think that's my line." She tightened her hold on the phone.

His rich baritone chuckle warmed Charisse like a summer breeze blowing off the waters of the Indian River—the estuary separating her hometown from Kennedy Space Center. "When can you start?"

Charisse swallowed. "When do you need me?"

Another loud cheer erupted, and Charisse pulled the phone from her ear as Gideon screamed in excitement. At least the office place would never be boring.

"Listen to that," he said. "Everyone's cheering because you're coming to work for me tomorrow morning at eight thirty."

Charisse covered her mouth to hide the mixture of horror, amusement, and the excitement of having her prayer answered so quickly.

"Are you there?" he asked.

She took her hand away. "Thank you, Gid." She cringed at the use of his nickname from long ago, but another round of enthusiastic cheering surely covered her mistake.

"You're welcome, Charisse. See you tomorrow."

Charisse put down the phone. *Gid!* What was she thinking? She needed to keep him at a distance—a very far and safe distance. If she didn't, she'd explode with the words that burned in her heart.

She closed her eyes against the memory of the young state attorney who came to her in the hall outside the courtroom to tell her of Gideon's ruling. While she stood there in stunned silence, the defendant, Carson Fullwell, walked from the courtroom. The man didn't even give her a second glance.

And Charisse's heart had broken anew.

Chapter Three

A knock woke Charisse from a good night's sleep. V.J. pushed the door open and ran to the edge of her bed. She reached out and straightened his Spiderman pajamas.

"Mommy, I have an idea." He bounced up and down in gleeful animation.

His smile flooded her heart with gratefulness. For the first time since she started working six weeks earlier, he was excited.

"What's your idea?" Charisse sat up. She'd agree to anything to keep that smile on his face.

"Can we go to Lake Eola for a picnic?"

"Gee. It's Saturday." She pushed the curtains by her bed aside, and peered out at the beautiful day. "And there's not a cloud in the blue sky."

"Mommy?" he begged.

"Well, maybe. On one condition."

His shoulders slumped. "I have to clean my room."

"Yeah, later, but if you'll give me a hug, *we* can clean your room when we get back from the park."

V.J. tackled her in a hug and then ran to dress. Charisse threw the covers off and hurried to get ready and pack a lunch. This would be a good day. She was sure of it.

Her enthusiasm dampened when she backed out of the garage and looked at her weed-infested yard with the overgrown shrubs. The pesky neighbors wouldn't be happy, but there was only so much she could do. And her migraine-producing allergies to the dust the lawnmower kicked up didn't help. V.J. did his best to weed the gardens, but time was limited. Given the choices of buying food, paying someone to mow her grass, or going to the doctor for allergy medication, she'd chosen the groceries.

Once at the park, Charisse forgot the yard. She and V.J. made their way through the crowd and spread the blanket on the grass as close as she could get to the playground, which was fenced by black wrought-iron. She placed a cooler on one corner and her box of picnic supplies on the other to anchor the cloth. V.J. stood on the blanket staring at the fountain in the middle of the lake. Then he turned and looked at the jungle gym and swings.

He swallowed and stared at her. She could almost read his mind. The last time they'd enjoyed the park Vance had taken him to the field to play catch. Later, they'd all romped around the playground. Then Vance rented one of the swan-shaped paddle boats. They laughed and carried on, enjoying the ride until her allergies kicked up, and she'd gotten an all-consuming migraine. She'd leaned her head against Vance as he singlehandedly paddled back to shore. V.J.'s little legs were too short to reach the pedals Charisse had abandoned.

Tears stung her eyes as Vance's words came to mind. "Times like today remind me why God entrusted you to me. I love you, Charisse, and I'd have paddled miles to see the smiles on both your faces."

Inhaling, she swatted away the tears. She'd taken Vance's sympathy and his kindness for granted.

V.J. sank to the corner of the blanket. "We should have invited Libby."

"Libby would love to be here, but her mother isn't feeling well, and we have the committee meeting tonight." Charisse walked to the sidewalk and pointed to the playground next to them. "Why don't we go play?"

V.J. shook his head. "Can I spend the night with Mamaw Taylor?" His gaze strayed across the park. Dogs romped with their owners, retrieving sticks, balls, and Frisbees. Kids at the park squealed with delight. Men and boys in t-shirts and ball caps played catch—like Vance had always done with their son.

"Sure, baby, but you'll miss church tomorrow." And she'd have to drive back to pick him up only to listen to her mother's next new reason why she should move back to Titusville and into her childhood home.

"I can go to church with Mamaw."

Charisse looked to the heavens. Not a cloud in the sky, but a heavy storm of emotion brewed in her heart. She hated spending time alone in the house without him, but she would never deprive him of something he enjoyed.

Feet trounced on the sidewalk, running in her direction. Charisse turned.

"Hey, I know you." Gideon came to a stop, but the large yellow lab on the leash had different plans. The dog lurched forward. "Cletus!" Gideon fell into her.

His arms encircled her as he pulled her toward him and rolled over, taking the brunt of the fall on the hard concrete sidewalk. Charisse fell against his chest with a jarring blow. The air pushed from her lungs.

"Mommy!" Her name fell from V.J.'s lips with alarm.

Gideon looked up at her as she tried to push off of his broad chest and gulp in air at the same time. "Charisse, are you okay? I'm sorry."

She held up her hand and nodded, settling on the ground beside him.

V.J. ran to her, but again the dog had a different idea. He jumped up on the little boy, his large paws resting on V.J.'s shoulders, pushing him down on his rump.

Charisse managed to suck enough air into her lungs to join in the laughter erupting from deep within V.J. as the dog covered him with kisses.

"Are you hurt?" Gideon looked her over, holding her shoulders between his warm hands. "Tell me I didn't hurt you."

"I'm okay, Gid," she said. "Nice of you to stumble upon us."

"I'd offer you a smirk, but I deserve much worse." Gideon wrapped his fist around the end of the leash and started to tug the dog away from V.J., but Charisse laid her hand on his and shook her head. Dog and boy wallowed on the ground, and little boy mirth filled the morning air.

Gideon pushed to his feet and bent to help her stand.

"You're bleeding." She reached for his elbow, cupping her hand over the wound dripping blood.

"It's nothing," he said.

Charisse rushed to her box of supplies and pulled out her paper towels. She tore a couple of sheets from the roll and tugged out a dishtowel she'd brought. She dipped the paper towels in the cooler and moved back to Gideon. "Let me see."

He held out his arm, and she squeezed the cold water over the injury and then pressed the wet towels against his elbow.

He winced and pulled away.

"Still a big baby, I see," she chided, and he held out his arm again.

She cleaned the scrape and wrapped the dishtowel around the wound.

"Thank you, Nurse Wellman." He smiled. "Should we rescue your son?"

Charisse took a deep breath and turned again to take in the sight of boy and dog.

Gideon pulled the lab back. "You must be V.J."

"Yes, sir." V.J. sat on his knees, peering up at Gideon.

"This is my boss, Judge Tabor," Charisse introduced.

V.J. gave an unenthusiastic wave of his hand. "Hi, Judge Tabor."

"And this unmannered specimen is my dog, Cletus."

Once more the dog pounced upon V.J. licking him relentlessly.

Charisse found a trash bag. She slipped the bloodied paper towels inside and plopped down on the blanket.

Gideon handed V.J. the leash. Without an invitation, Gideon fell onto the blanket beside her and shrugged off the backpack he carried. "Doesn't smile much since his daddy's death?" he whispered.

Charisse shook her head and continued to watch. "Very little." No need to tell Gideon he hadn't helped their healing process any with his off-the-wall ruling.

"When I lost Dad in high school, it took the wind out of me." He studied her makeshift bandage.

She opened her mouth to tell him she remembered but clamped it shut.

Gideon's eyes rested on her son. "Other than the whole collision thing, I'm glad I ran into you. I've been meaning to tell you what a wonderful job you're doing." He brushed the sand from his shorts and top. "I know Delilah is a handful, but you never let her ruffle you."

"Oh, there's a difference in her ruffling me and my letting her know she does."

"Thanks for putting up with her. If you came to me and told me you were quitting, it would be a sad day. You've been a tremendous help. I think it's a shame you weren't able to continue law school."

"Someday." She stared out at the lake and the swan boats filled with couples and families. Biting into her lower lip, she told herself she wouldn't let Gideon see what he'd brought her to, the hopelessness she felt without her husband.

Someday would probably never come. She needed to support her son, and V.J. still held to his grief. The school counselors and V.J.'s teachers had been nice enough to point that out to her on a number of occasions. Adding law school to her schedule would take her away from him even more than her job was doing.

"I feel blessed, though, to have you in my corner," Gideon said.

She must be hiding her feelings well. On occasion, she'd even been able to forget what Gideon had done. "Well, thank you for saying so. I'm actually enjoying my work. Judge Foster and I have become fast friends, and Zelma is a hoot."

Gideon glanced at her, his lips playing with a smile. What had she said to amuse him?

Gideon leaned into her with his shoulder, nudging her a bit. "I used to love the way you pulled out archaic words."

Charisse shook her head. She had no desire to relive any of her past with him.

Gideon nodded toward the dog and boy. V.J. and Cletus lay on their sides. Cletus's front paws rested on V.J.'s shoulders. Cletus's tongue hung out the side of his mouth. V.J. rubbed the dog's nose.

Gideon whistled and the dog scrambled up and ran to him. He flipped open his backpack and pulled out a Frisbee before unleashing Cletus. "V.J., how'd you like to help me out and give Cletus some exercise? Can you throw a Frisbee?"

"Yes, sir." V.J. jumped up.

Cletus's eyes followed the Frisbee in Gideon's hand.

"Don't throw it too far. He's pretty single-minded when it comes to catch, but you never know when a pretty girl dog might catch his attention."

V.J. giggled again. "We don't like girls, do we, boy?" He took the Frisbee and tossed it. Cletus bounded after it, returned, and dropped it at V.J.'s feet. "Look, Mommy.

He's smart." V.J. threw the Frisbee again and ran with the dog. Cletus beat him to the toy. He stood with his paw covering it. When V.J. reached down for it, Cletus grabbed the toy and wrestled him for control.

V.J. released the Frisbee and returned to his original spot. Cletus followed, dropping the toy at his feet.

"He is pretty smart." Charisse leaned back.

"He's trained me pretty well." Gideon rested his arms on his knees.

"Do you live downtown?" she asked.

"I have a condo in the Waverly. You?"

She laughed. "Wow, Gid. How do you rate?"

He stared at her for a long moment without giving her a clue of his thoughts.

She lowered her head. "I'm sorry."

"You're always so formal. We knew each other before I ever thought of practicing law or dreamed I'd be appointed to the bench. Will you remember to call me Gid and not Judge Tabor?"

"I don't think—" Yet, she just did.

"You're smarter than Delilah. You know when formality is important, but if you ever call me Giddy, I don't care how valuable you are, I'll fire you."

She nodded. She'd never call him by that hideous moniker Delilah James stuck upon him—even it if would be a small sort of vengeance.

"And to answer your question, I got a deal on my condo. Short sale." He winked. "So where do you and V.J. call home?"

"Off Summerlin Avenue. What type of law did you practice before becoming a judge?"

"A little of everything, including criminal law. Real estate and probate mainly. How do you think I got such a good deal on my condo?" The corners of his eyes crinkled with his huge smile.

V.J. ran after Cletus again and the two tugged at the Frisbee. Cletus pulled then stopped, never letting up the tension.

Gideon touched her shoulder. "Watch Cletus."

V.J. continued to hold to the Frisbee. He yanked once. Cletus snatched back. V.J. pulled back again, and the dog let go. The boy tumbled over backward, and Cletus ran to him, licking V.J.'s face while V.J. begged for mercy.

"I promised Cletus an ice cream. Do you care if I treat V.J.?"

Charisse watched her son play with Gideon's dog. Everything within her screamed that she needed to push Gideon aside, but V.J.'s mood had changed from dour to joyful since Gideon's arrival, though she'd give all the credit to Cletus and none to his master.

"Why not? This is a day made to eat dessert first. I know he'd love to walk with you. I can fix our lunch while you're gone. You'll picnic with us?" Not asking him would be rude. And after all, it wouldn't pay to be discourteous to her boss.

"I'd love to, Charisse. Thank you." Gideon jumped to his feet and whistled.

Cletus looked up then gave V.J. one more lick before running to Gideon. "We're going for ice cream, Veej. Your mom said you could go. Want to walk with us?"

"Really?" V.J. stopped in front of Charisse, searching her face.

"If you promise to keep Judge Tabor out of trouble."

"What would you like, Charisse?" Gideon clipped the leash onto Cletus's collar and held out his hand for V.J. "One of those strawberry shortcake ice cream bars you used to love?"

She shook her head, not willing to give him kudos for remembering. "It'll melt. You enjoy."

"A slushie? Maybe a candy bar?"

"No. I'm fine." She managed to hold off the tears of gratitude until man, boy, and dog disappeared around the corner.

Gideon waited his turn and took a wet wipe from Charisse. He swabbed the sticky ice cream from his hands and mouth.

V.J. sat between them, and Charisse handed him a plate with a peanut butter and jelly sandwich and chips.

"Yummy." Gideon took the plate she offered to him. "I haven't had a P, B, and J in years."

"We eat a lot of them lately," Charisse said and then shook her head. "They're our favorite, huh, V.J.?"

V.J. nodded. "And macaroni and cheese."

"Ramen noodles, too, I bet." Gideon lifted a brow.

Charisse didn't smile at his lame joke. In law school, on a limited budget, his diet primarily consisted of mac and cheese and Ramen noodles. Maybe his words hit too close to home. He thought she'd been crying when they

Charisse

returned, but now her pert little nose turned pink, and he was sure of it. Her vulnerability tugged at him, reminding him of the girl he'd known in high school. "Do you have any plans for this evening?"

Charisse straightened. "I—yes. I have a reunion meeting."

"Well, maybe another time. I was thinking of having dinner at the Citrus. Having company would have been nice." No need to tell her he ate there most evenings.

She looked away.

"Veej, where do you go to school?"

"Hillcrest," V.J. spoke with his mouth full.

"Mind your manners, young man," Charisse warned, her voice tight with emotion.

V.J. swallowed. "Yes, ma'am. Judge Tabor, how did you teach Cletus to play Frisbee?"

"He taught me." Gideon laughed. "I saw him teaching you a few of his tricks."

"He's a cool dog. I wish we had one."

"I think he wishes he had one of you, too."

Charisse rewarded him for his joke with a soft laugh.

"I'll tell you what, Veej. Cletus has me on a tight schedule. When I'm not doing weekend court, we're here every Saturday morning. You and your mom are welcome to join me."

V.J. bounced on his knees. "Can we, Mommy? Can we?"

Charisse narrowed her eyes in Gideon's direction. What had he done?

"Can we?" V.J. repeated, his hands clasped in front of him as if in prayer.

Charisse's tight features softened, and she leaned forward and placed her hands on each side of V.J.'s rosy cheeks. "I'd love to, silly boy. Anything that makes you this happy has to be good for both of us." She hugged V.J. to her and looked at Gideon. "Thank you," she mouthed.

He nodded and bit into his sandwich. "So, Veej, Mommy tells me you like sports. Do you play soccer?" Didn't every kid play soccer?

"Mommy says it isn't an American sport."

Gideon choked on his food. "Really? You're still saying that?"

"It's not American." She laughed at the old joke they used to share.

"Well, you used to play at tennis." He winked. "I think it began in France. Would you limit us to football, baseball, and basketball?"

"Play at?" She smacked his arm and then pulled back. Pain flitted across her face. "I guess I could only play at it back then. I was a little too heavy to cross court."

Gideon kept his mouth shut. He could tell her she was beautiful in high school—just as knock-out gorgeous as she was now, but that would probably be a step over the line.

"Something wrong, Judge Tabor?" Charisse asked.

He shook his head. Charisse was an enigma. Since she'd begun working for him, he suspected any kindness she rendered to him was forced. But it always came back to her smile following the interview. The turn of her lips had seemed genuine. She'd meant it when she told him it was good to see him, but since that day, she maintained a very professional relationship. He wanted to get beyond it somehow, to claim their old friendship. "Call me Gid," he said, but she cast a quick glance in V.J.'s direction.

Careful.

If he didn't watch it, he'd give away his deepest secret. He'd always been in love with her. "So tell me. How's the reunion planning going?" Perhaps a change of subject would keep his mind off his growing desires.

He looked to where V.J. romped with Cletus. Desire didn't always come in a neatly wrapped package. He craved the feel of Charisse in his arms. He'd give anything to whisper in her ear and tell her he'd vanquish her every worry.

But Charisse came with a son. He'd never thought of a ready-made family, but who wouldn't want to protect and raise V.J.? His father must have been quite a man.

Gideon always wanted kids—nine or ten—but time was passing him by. Spending these few hours with Charisse and her boy speared him with the truth. He wasn't getting any younger. "How about tomorrow night?" He chomped down on his last bite of sandwich. "Dinner?"

"To answer your first question, the reunion planning is going well. To answer your second question, we have church tomorrow night."

Gideon shook his head. "I've got a lot on my mind." Not a lie. She didn't need to know his every thought was about her. "And, yeah, tomorrow's Sunday. I forgot, and I promised to help with a program at Deacon's church." He pushed down the disappointment. "Another time, maybe." No reason to make her think him needy.

Charisse began to clean up their plates, putting the trash into a bag. V.J. took it from her and ran to a nearby trashcan.

"Are you okay?" He finally had the opportunity to ask.

Charisse bit her lip and nodded.

"Because you don't look like you are. I'm thinking you're pretty close to the edge."

"Surprisingly, our accidental meeting pulled me away from the ledge. You and Cletus worked wonders."

"Can I help? Do you need someone to watch him while you attend your meeting?"

V.J. grabbed the Frisbee, and the boy and dog began to romp again.

"No, he's looking forward to staying with my mother. He said he wanted to spend the night with her."

"That's good. How is your mom?"

"Never changes."

He hated to hear that. Her mom was on the demanding side. Gideon always thought Mrs. Taylor's strictness the reason Charisse cowered from conflict during high school.

"We get along better with distance between us, but she loves to spend time with V.J."

"How'd you lose your husband?"

She jerked her gaze to his. Her body tensed and just as soon her shoulders folded. "An *accident.*"

Why did he feel as if she was hiding something from him? "On the job, at home, in a car?"

"Gid, I don't want to talk about it."

In unguarded moments, his name flowed so easily from her lips. He usually liked the sound of it, but this time it dripped with disdain. He chose to ignore her tone. "Well, anytime you need someone to babysit, let me know. Cletus and I could use the company."

Her eyes overflowed with tears, and she nodded. "He'd enjoy that."

He reached up and wiped the streaming rivulets from her face. "Charisse, I think you could use some company, too."

She leaned into his touch but then pulled away with a gasp.

"I'm sorry." He jumped to his feet.

He could keep Charisse Wellman as one of the best law clerks he'd ever find, or he could pursue her, break through her defenses, and try to make her fall in love with him. But with her penetrating glare and the sudden movement to put distance between them, he knew he couldn't do both.

He had a law clerk tough enough to put up with Delilah James.

He planned to keep her.

FAY LAMB

Chapter Four

Charisse ran into the Titusville library carrying her notebook, purse, and plans for the setup and decorations at Royal Oak Country Club. "I'm sorry. I had an appointment at the country club to review some details, and I lost track of time." She was habitually late and forever asking Libby to forgive her for taking precious moments away from her ailing mother.

Karen Greely, the reunion committee chairperson smiled, and her blue eyes twinkled with amusement. "For you, Charisse, fifteen minutes late is actually five minutes early."

Charisse laughed and pulled out a chair and sat. "Then I'm glad to, for once, arrive before I should."

These were her kind of folks. None of the women in this group were popular during high school. Karen called the shots as a well-known city councilwoman. After graduation, Pearl ended up attending the same college as Gideon's favorite receiver, Roger Wright. These days she was a housewife with three kids. Debbie York never married, and she waitressed for Titusville's most popular attraction, Dixie Crossroads, a seafood restaurant run by a multi-generational Titusville family. Libby worked part time at a garden nursery whose owners allowed her time off when she needed to care for her mother.

"Libby, how many RSVPs do we have?" Karen leaned forward, hands clasped.

"A quarter of the class—fifty-five so far. Add spouses and dates, and we're looking at a hundred to a hundred ten people."

"That's a good turnout." Karen nodded. "Reunions are usually held in the summer. We're doing this in conjunction with the inductions and school anniversary, and several classes who graduated in years close to ours are taking part. Still, that's a larger number attending the dinner than I estimated."

Charisse chewed on the tip of her pen. "I think the former athletes are the draw. Even those already inducted will be giving speeches for the coaches and the players being honored. People will attend to see them."

"Is there a certain quarterback you can't wait to see?" Pearl nudged Charisse.

Charisse forced a laugh. She hadn't even told Libby she worked for Gideon, convincing herself that if she kept the truth to herself the traitorous action would seem less real.

The ladies were staring at her. She had to come up with an answer. "Oh, there are one or two other fellows on the team who used to dissuade others from telling fat jokes about me. Your husband was one of them."

"Has Gideon Tabor responded?" Karen eyed Libby.

Libby pinched her lips together, a sure sign she didn't like the others picking on Charisse. She perused the slips of paper in front of her and pulled out one. Charisse recognized Gideon's signature. "He did." Libby cast Charisse an apologetic glance.

"Is he bringing a date?" Debbie leaned forward. "He can't be single."

Charisse's heart stilled. She hadn't thought about Gideon attending with a date. What if he brought Judge Delilah with him? If he planned to escort that vixen, Charisse sure wouldn't take part in the festivities.

How could she think this way?

"He only RSVP'd for one." Libby shook her head. "Don't be teasing Charisse. She's long over Gideon Tabor. And look at you all. Two of you are married."

"He was a nice guy," Pearl said. "Roger can't wait to see him again. Gideon only lives in Orlando, you know. I'm surprised you two haven't run into each other."

Charisse squirmed in her seat. She'd always been taught silence was only another form of mistruth. What would be the harm in telling them? No matter what he'd done, his actions since he'd hired her had been beyond reproach. Hers on the other hand—leaning into his touch like a love-starved woman—had horrified her. Nope. She'd keep it to herself.

"He's a judge. Gideon Tabor, can you believe it?" Pearl continued.

Charisse turned. "What's so hard to believe about that?"

"How can you ask such a question? You spent four years of high school tutoring him."

Yes she had, but sometimes she wondered why she had to tutor him at all. Often now, he took the time to teach her, saying it was something she'd need to know in law school once she returned. She'd learned over the last six weeks that Gideon was a smart, commonsense man with compassion and honor.

Honor? What am I saying? He allowed a killer to go free.

"Maybe he had trouble in the classroom setting," Libby said. "We're not here to beat up on Gideon Tabor. Praise God he worked hard to get through law school and to become a judge."

Charisse offered her mediating friend a smile. "I spoke with the manager at Royal Oak Country Club." She pulled her glasses from her purse and slid them on her face. Then she slid out a sketch from her notebook. "The manager confirmed the third Saturday in April—that's only four weeks out. The buffet will offer roast beef and chicken entrees." She placed the diagram in the middle of the table. "I think this seating will be fine. The manager said no problem."

Karen pulled the paper toward her. "I know a few people who plan to crash the event. With the reunion and induction going on at the same time, I don't know how we can tell them no. They won't show for dinner, but they'll be there to hang out afterward. We'll need the extra seating. Good job, Charisse."

"A lady from my church loves to bake for weddings and events. She's agreed to design a cake in the shape of our War Eagle emblem, and she isn't charging us a thing," Libby said.

"Too cool," Debbie said. "That's great, Libby."

"Good. I didn't ask Royal Oak to provide a dessert with the buffet." Charisse noted Libby's information in her notebook.

Libby reached and brought Charisse's seating chart toward her. "Karen and I retrieved a box of old photographs from Dick Majors. Remember him, the yearbook editor for our class? We're going through them. We plan to have a wall of memories. Can we place it here in the center?" She pointed. "People will have fun walking around both sides to see the pics."

"I don't see why not. Wow, Libby, great thinking." Charisse raised her brows.

"Our Libby is quite the event planner," Karen complimented.

The color on Libby's face deepened. She looked at her watch. "Is there anything else we need to cover?"

Debbie raised her hand and put it down. "I'm having a friend print out the nametags, the embossed napkins, and some novelty cups with our class information on it. A few companies owned by alumni are donating door prizes. One could be a cruise."

"Now, that will have to be a special giveaway," Karen said.

When the meeting ended, Charisse and Libby gathered up their papers. After a few polite words and jokes in farewell, they walked out together. "You okay?"

"Momma's not doing well. We're doing our best to keep her out of the hospital."

"I'm sorry, Libby."

Libby's shoulders fell. "The doctor will probably send her to Orlando again."

Charisse rubbed her arms against March's chilly breeze. She leaned against her car and looked at Libby.

"If they do, why don't you plan to spend some time with me and V.J.?"

"I might look you up for lunch, but I don't like to leave her alone too long."

"I'll visit her. Seems the only time I see her anymore is when she's in the hospital."

"But she looks forward to your visits." Libby touched Charisse's arm. "I'm sorry about the girls. If they knew about the trial, they wouldn't have said a thing."

Charisse nodded and looked to the ground.

Libby leaned against the car sharing a comforting silence. Charisse didn't want to tell her friend she worked for the enemy, that her emotions warred every day with demanding the truth from Gideon.

At last, Charisse pushed away from her car.

Libby did the same. "Be careful going home."

"Libby, I think someone needs a hug." Charisse engulfed her in a tight embrace.

"I did need that. Thank you." Libby smiled.

"I was talking about me." Charisse laughed and turned to her car as Libby swatted at her. Charisse brought her arm back to her side, palm clenched upward. With perfection, she'd pulled off a Gideon Tabor move.

And the fact she'd done it irked her.

Gideon stared out the window of the Citrus Restaurant. The city lights showcased Orlando's rich architectural heritage. Even an overpass across the street did little to diminish the character of downtown. People strolled past him. Others ate at tables along the sidewalk in front of the eatery.

Gideon had been sitting outside until Delilah walked by and insisted upon joining him, but only if he moved inside with her. He should have declined and remained at his table.

This wasn't how he pictured dinner when he'd asked Charisse and her son to join him. Instead of gazing at the natural beauty of Charisse Wellman he found himself sitting across from Delilah, who was dressed to the hilt, makeup applied like a runway model, ready for some gala she planned to attend. His only consolation was he'd made it this far into the meal without war breaking out between them and without the restaurant's staff practicing their knife-throwing skills in their direction. The last time he'd dined here with Delilah, he was convinced the auburn-haired waitress held a blade at her side, ready to plunge it into Delilah's sarcastic soul if she made one more untoward remark.

Gideon waved off dessert, but Delilah loved her sweets, and her downfall was carrot cake. Of course, the woman worked out seven days a week, and he guessed she should enjoy a little of the good stuff once in a while.

The blonde waitress approaching with Delilah's cake did so like a mouse approaching a cat with an offering of cheese.

Gideon offered the young woman a smile. No use telling her Delilah's claws would remain retracted—the cake a better treat than any random sarcasm Delilah could bestow.

The waitress put the plate down, jerking her hand back. Good thing. Delilah stabbed the cake and brought a bite to her mouth. "Hmmm, good."

"Thank you," Gideon said as the girl put the ticket on the table. He pulled out his debit card and handed it to her. The waitress picked it up and skedaddled.

"Don't leave her a big tip. She was horrible." Delilah spoke with her mouth full.

Charisse had admonished her son when he'd done the same thing during lunch at the park. A smile tugged at the corner of Gideon's lips. What a pair—mother and son.

"What's so amusing?" Delilah swallowed her bite of cake and sipped her coffee.

"I ran into Charisse Wellman and her son in the park today. I thought of something that frankly didn't strike me as humorous until now."

"Oh, yeah, what did Ms. Wonderful do?" Delilah's legs were crossed, and she swung her right leg under the table, her stiletto heel catching against his pants leg each time.

He'd gone and made her mad.

Good.

He moved his leg out of the line of her torture. "I had a good time. That's all. Her son is a great kid."

"And he has a father, right?"

"Really, Dee?" Gideon sat back as the waitress returned. He opened the bill, included a substantial tip, and signed the slip. "She's worked in the office for well over a month. She does most of your clerk's work, and you haven't even thought to ask her about her life?"

"I'm too busy."

"Yeah, I see that. Ask Crystal to stop imposing on Charisse, will you? I keep her busy enough. Let Marlene help with the copies. That's what the receptionist is supposed to do, and I think Marlene's a little offended that her work has been taken from her."

"A little protective of her, are we, Giddy?"

"Marlene? Yeah. She's a great girl, real eager to learn." He tilted his head back and moved it one way then the other while rubbing his neck. How could he have been so relaxed in the park with Charisse and be so tense here with Delilah?

"You're bleeding." Delilah pointed toward his elbow with her fork. "Nasty."

Gideon looked at the dried stain on his white shirt. If it had been Charisse sitting across from him, he was sure his sleeve would be rolled back and a makeshift bandage reapplied. He slipped his dinner napkin from his lap and staunched the already clotting flow.

Delilah finished her cake and pushed the plate aside. "I was talking about Ms. Wonderful. You never protected Stacey like this. Did Charisse take advantage of your little meeting in the park to voice her displeasure?"

"Delilah, the woman has more to worry about than your little games. I'm asking you to back away. I'm sure if I don't keep her busy enough, she'll offer to help Crystal."

Delilah peered at him over the rim of her coffee cup. "Giddy, you're not getting involved with her, are you—a married woman with a kid? I mean, your Christianity isn't in the balance here, is it?"

He hated her constant use of the horrible nickname she'd pegged him with, and he despised the way she took every chance to belittle his faith. Still he was thankful Delilah hadn't zeroed in on the fact that he and Charisse were old friends.

"Charisse is a widow with a young son," he corrected. "And I ran into her at the park today. I hung around to let her son play with Cletus. End of story."

A story that started long ago.

"I should hope so." She narrowed her eyes. "Never a good idea to get involved with the office staff. Not good for political gain."

"And what would you call this little meeting." Gideon stood, tucking his wallet into his back pocket. "I've known for a while our meetings here aren't by chance."

"This isn't the same. We're not staff. We're two educated equals. You're looking beneath your status, unless …" She narrowed her eyes. "You aren't telling me the type of woman you want is a little homemaker, someone who'll have cookies and milk for you and the children when you walk in the door after a hard day in court?"

Gideon leaned down, his palms flat against the table. "What I want in a woman is none of your business, Delilah James, but since you've opened up this line of questioning, let me give you some rebuttal. The type of woman I'd like for a wife, if I ever find her, will be compassionate toward people. She won't worry about status. She'll be welcome to have any career she wants so long as God and her family take precedence over that endeavor. And most of all, she won't embarrass me every time I find myself dining with her."

"Good luck finding that woman." Delilah waved her nearly empty cup in the air as if his words had no impact, but a momentary glint of understanding flitted across her face.

"I did find her once, and I was too much of a stupid kid to notice." He pushed from the table. "Delilah, I want to be your friend, but we're never going to be anything more."

"Who said I want a big oaf like you?" The cup in her hand shook as she emptied it. She cleared her throat after forcing the coffee down. "Why don't you join me tonight? It's Saturday after all."

"I have church tomorrow, but thanks for the offer. Be careful." He walked outside.

Lately, spending any amount of time with Delilah left him grouchy. Deacon would tell him it was conviction. Gideon shrugged it off as pure exasperation.

And now he could tell Deacon that setting the record straight didn't make him feel any better. He'd hurt Delilah. Who knew that was possible? Apparently, she did feel something for him, though he doubted it was anything lasting or meaningful.

He looked at his watch. Nine o'clock. Too late to call Deacon. He'd have to talk this over with Cletus when he got home.

Chapter Five

Charisse tossed her purse under the desk and turned on her computer. She took a deep breath to calm her frayed nerves. A blossoming headache threatened to turn into a full-blown migraine, and she rubbed her temples in an attempt to persuade it to go away.

"Charisse!" Gideon roared before she could sit down.

He never bellowed like that, and she had no idea what she could have done. She walked across the hall. "Good morning." Not that she'd had one. The look on his face told her it wouldn't get any better either.

Gideon didn't look up as he plundered his desk. "I gave you research on the Jefferson case, my one o'clock hearing. I promised a decision today. Do you have it done?"

"You never asked me to do research on the Jefferson case," she answered. "But if you'll give me the information—"

"You've got to be kidding. It's a month's worth of research. I mentioned that when I gave it to you. You stood right beside my chair, looking over my shoulder, and even admitted it would take a while."

Charisse leaned forward and placed her palms on Gideon's desk. V.J.'s early morning temper tantrum left her drained, and now she had to deal with this. "Judge

Tabor, I don't remember your request for research. It's been on your calendar, yes, but I believe it was set before I started working for you."

And when had she ever leaned over his shoulder?

"At least get me something I can use. I believe my ruling should favor the defendant. I pulled a few cases backing my decision, but I want the most recent." He handed her his case law and the court file, shaking his head as she took them. "I can't believe you forgot this."

Rationalizing with him would get her nowhere. She'd left a little boy at school and arrived at work to face a spoiled baby. "I'll do my best."

"Your best would have meant getting it to me on Friday."

Before she could speak, Gideon opened another file, ignoring her.

Charisse moved to the doorway and stood looking at him. On Saturday, he'd been full of nothing but praise for her. Angry words played in her mind. Her probationary period continued for another thirty days. Opening her mouth and telling him what she thought of him at this moment would ruin her chances of keeping her job, and she'd only now begun to dig herself out from under the financial strain crushing her.

To think she'd told V.J. she couldn't attend his show-and-tell presentation tomorrow. For what? A boss who majored in *jerkology*.

She stormed into her office and closed the door.

"Charisse." She jumped at the buzz of the telephone. "Your son's school, line two."

Charisse rubbed tired eyes, punched the line, and used the speaker. "Charisse Wellman."

"Ms. Wellman, this is Nurse Caldwell at Hillcrest."

"Is V.J. all right?"

"Nothing serious. He's lethargic. Could be nothing but he could be coming down with something as well."

Charisse tilted her head and stared at the ceiling. After all the meetings with the principal, the phone calls from the school's counselor, and the teacher's numerous notes, they still didn't understand: V.J. was a little boy who missed his father.

"I have him in the clinic waiting for your arrival."

"I can't leave work right away, but I'll be able to pick him up in a half hour. Will he be okay until then?"

"He'll be fine. He's sleeping now."

"Thank you." She pushed the button to end the call.

Tears welled in her eyes as she turned to her computer. Gid never asked her to do this research. *Lord. It's unfair that I have to take the blame.*

Her office door swung open. "There are twenty cases listed in the Petitioner's Memorandum of Law. I want them pulled and on my desk by five o'clock." Judge James slapped the pleading onto Charisse's desk and walked out the door. She turned and glared at Charisse and then entered Gideon's chambers before Charisse could explain she needed to leave. Besides, the attorneys were supposed to attach their case law to their memorandums.

Complaining would do no good, and it would only give Delilah ammunition to use against her. Charisse reached for her purse to pull out some aspirin for the growing headache.

"You don't work for her, you know."

Charisse swiveled in her chair and faced her visitor. "How are you, Judge Foster?" She dug in her purse and pulled out the pill bottle, opened it, and poured two aspirin into her hand. She popped them in her mouth and swallowed them without water.

"I'm fine, Ms. Charisse, and you don't have to put up with her."

Normally, Charisse loved the brief snatches of time she spent with the older judge. His southernisms made her feel right at home. She'd pegged him as a Florida cracker, what Floridians called the natives, from their first meeting—something they had in common. He doted on her and though she couldn't say for sure, Charisse thought he stood guard between her and the brash female who'd dumped the work on her desk. "Judge James doesn't bother me."

Judge Foster shook his head. "And you don't realize how much you bother her, do you?"

"Now, why would I bother her?"

"Because she can't ruffle your feathers."

Gideon had mentioned that on Saturday—the other Gideon—the one her turncoat mind brought into her dreams last night. The man in his office today was a monster clone—the man she'd imagined he'd become since the day he kept the door open on her closure of her husband's death.

She'd not be having those dreams again.

Charisse

A half hour turned into two hours. Charisse's hands shook as she entered the keywords into the database. V.J. needed her. She needed to get the job done. Her hands continued to type the wrong letters, and she backspaced not once, not twice, but three times. "Lord, I can't do this." *I'm being torn apart. I wanted to give V.J. a better life by taking this job. Now, he feels as if I've abandoned him, and today he might be right. I'm working for an ungrateful idiot. I'm ready to leave and not come back. Please, show me what to do.*

The buzzer sounded. "Charisse, line two."

What else could happen? "This is Charisse. May I help you?"

"This may seem like a very odd call, but my name is Stacey. I worked for Gideon before you."

"Okay."

"I don't know why this popped into my head, but Gideon had a hearing on his calendar for today. I can't remember the time, but I recall it was very important to him. I prepared some research."

"Yes?" Charisse leaned forward.

"Have you run across a file folder in your side drawer?"

Charisse jerked the drawer open and rummaged through it.

"I think I labeled it, but I can't remember the case name. It's funny the hearing came to mind. I do recall how much Gideon wanted to render the correct ruling. Divine providence, huh?"

"The file is Jefferson." Charisse pulled the folder out and held it up to declare victory. "Stacey, I love you. I owe you big time." *And Lord, thank You for reminding me of Your goodness.*

"Glad I could help," Stacey said. "I'm sorry, what's your name?"

"Charisse."

"Charisse, don't let Judge Delilah run you off. Gideon's a good guy. You won't find a better boss."

"Why'd you leave?" Charisse couldn't help but ask.

Stacey laughed. "I had a baby and left to raise him and my husband."

Charisse clutched the phone and closed her eyes. The memories of her own cherished time when she had that same job came crashing through her walls of strength.

"Good luck, Charisse. Stay tough. Sometimes Gideon can act like a big baby, but he makes up for it," Stacey said.

"Thank you. If you ever get downtown, please let me buy you lunch. I owe you."

"Don't think anything of it." Stacey hung up.

Charisse leafed through the file and ran a search on the database. Satisfied Stacey's work was still valid and contained most of the information she'd dug up, she headed across the hall to Gideon's office and knocked on the door. The monster clone was a dead man.

No answer. She rapped again.

"He and Judge Foster went to lunch about an hour ago." Marlene hung up from a call.

Charisse

Charisse pushed the door open and dropped the file on Gideon's chair where he would be sure to find it. "I have to go." She stomped out of his office.

"Line three, your son's school. Let me help you with something."

"Can you pull and copy some case law for me?" Charisse reached over the receptionist's desk and pushed the button. "Ms. Caldwell, I'm on my way."

"Your son has been waiting for his mother for several hours."

"You told me V.J. was lethargic and asleep."

"Two hours ago, yes."

"I'm on my way." She pushed the button. "My son isn't feeling well, Marlene. Judge James left a Memorandum of Law on my desk. If you could start copying the cases the attorney cites, it would be a big help. Thank you."

She met a human wall as she turned. Stepping back, she looked up into Gideon's green eyes. They held a softness she hadn't expected, but she wasn't about to forgive him so easily.

"Veej sick?" he asked.

She shook her head. "No, he seemed tired, and they thought it was a good excuse for him to miss class. I need to go." She stepped around him. "I'll be back in one hour. I haven't taken my lunch yet."

"Why don't you bring him back here?"

Charisse stopped and studied him. "He's a seven-year-old kid. The three hours I'll have remaining in my work day will seem an eternity to him, but I may accept your offer." She rushed down the hall.

"Charisse," he called to her as she stood at the elevator door. "My hearing?"

"Stacey called. She told me where to locate the research you asked *her* to do. I reviewed it, and everything seems in order. It's on your chair." She refused to look at him as she stepped onto the elevator.

Gideon stared out the window watching Charisse cross the busy street, her little boy holding her hand. With the other hand, she swiped back the stands of her hair that the wind blew across her beautiful face.

"Giddy, will you kindly explain to Deacon I'm well within my rights to go outside the sentencing guidelines if I think it's warranted."

Behind him Deacon harrumphed. "If it's warranted. That's my entire argument. The guy has no priors. He messed up one time. And don't be tellin' me if you were bein' impartial you'd not give him a lesser sentence. You don't like his attorney."

Delilah sighed with exaggerated finesse. "If his attorney thought so, I imagine he'd seek Gideon out to ask him to do his bidding instead of you. After all, John Turner is Gideon's friend."

"'Nuff said," Deacon chided.

"Giddy," Delilah demanded.

"Huh?" He continued to pretend to ignore his colleagues and gaze at the street a few stories below. Charisse stooped in front of V.J. before entering the building, and the little one nodded at every word she said.

She pulled her son into her embrace and then stood. They disappeared from view.

Gideon turned his attention to the bickering in his office, though he'd had enough arguing in the courtroom. Stacey and Charisse's research had shut the state attorney down, and he was able to find for the defendant and get out of the courtroom quickly.

"What has your attention?" Delilah stepped toward the window.

Only to aggravate her, Gideon barred Delilah's view, but his eyes rested upon Deacon who plopped into the chair in front of the desk.

"What are you two arguing over?" Gideon asked. He heard, but he also hoped they'd drop the bickering.

Deacon shrugged.

"I've just received a lecture from Deacon about sentencing guidelines."

"Ah, what's the use?" Deacon waved her off. "Keep on goin' like you're a goin', and the Florida Bar will back someone else. Isn't that how you got elected in the first place? You showed 'em your snake-like charm."

"Look, I'm not a good-old Florida boy like you. I needed some backing."

"Well, you ain't gonna keep 'em on your side with off-the-wall sentences. For your information, Turner didn't say a word. I heard a bunch of lawyers talkin' about it after court. Seems you made quite the impression, and a not so good one at that."

Delilah placed her hands on her hips. Her smile told him she thought Gideon would render her a favorable opinion.

"Okay, children. Let's call a truce. Deacon, Delilah is entitled to all the bad decisions she wants to make."

"You rat." Delilah turned away from Gideon to glare at Deacon.

"Speaking of being a rat, why'd you go and drop all that work on Ms. Charisse's desk?" Deacon baited the hook for another argument.

Gideon shot him a warning gaze. He wasn't up to fishing for piranha today.

Charisse walked into her office across the hall, her son following behind, and Gideon turned his attention to her. She stopped at her desk, pressing her palm to her eyes for a moment before giving V.J. instructions and pointing to a chair.

"Did she complain to you, Deacon?" Delilah asked.

"Does she appear to be the type of woman who'd complain?" Deacon shot back.

"No, she doesn't." Gideon stepped away from the window and grinned as Delilah peered downward. "Delilah, I asked you not to give Charisse extra work. She has more than enough to keep her busy. Clear any work you give her through me."

"Fine." Delilah moved from the window and stood beside him. Her hand rested on his shoulder as she looked through his open office door.

Deacon turned in his chair. "That her boy?"

Gideon nodded. "V.J. He's not feeling well."

"And she brought him here to spread his germs?" Delilah huffed.

As if on cue, V.J. sneezed.

"All over the place." Gideon stood and pushed by Delilah. "Excuse me."

Charisse stapled the last of the copies together and placed them into the folder. She looked at her watch. Panic struck as she realized how long she'd left V.J. alone in her office. She should have known. Delilah never gave her any easy assignments. Those she reserved for Crystal.

Marlene apologized for not getting to the work, but when the phone wasn't ringing, Crystal had her making calls and running back and forth to the copy machine, keeping Charisse from making the copies for Crystal's boss.

The twenty cases listed in the attorney's pleading proved obscure at best, and Charisse had trouble locating each one.

While she and Marlene slaved over the work Delilah doled out, Crystal took three breaks. Charisse chalked up her frustration to the fact V.J. was his usual self. The half day of class he missed was unnecessary, and the nurse gave her no reasoning behind the school's actions. She'd indicated V.J.'s teacher would call Charisse at home this evening.

Charisse couldn't wait.

She hurried down the hall and entered Crystal's office. "Here you go." She forced a smile.

Crystal shrugged, and Charisse stepped out into the hallway. Why hadn't she listened to Gid and refused to do the work?

Because the big baby was in a mood, and who knew if he remembered what he'd declared to her on Saturday?

Charisse opened her office door. "V.J., just a little—" She stopped.

Her son was gone.

"V.J.," she whispered, fear spreading through her like medicine injected into her vein. She shouldn't have brought him with her. Too many people—some of them bad people with arrests for wicked things—came through the courthouse doors.

Marlene, talking to a caller on the phone, waved at Charisse from behind the receptionist's desk and pointed toward Gideon's partially opened door.

Charisse couldn't deal with him. She had to find V.J.

"My son is missing." She stepped out of her office. "Have you seen him?"

Marlene put her finger to her lips and pointed toward Gideon's office again.

Charisse stepped forward, peering around the corner. An unexpected sight drew her into the room like a chance glimpse at a beautiful painting.

Gideon and V.J. were sprawled on the floor with a large sketch board and the cars and trucks used in courtroom testimony to depict accident scenes. Together, they'd created a city of streets and buildings, and on the roads they rolled the miniature vehicles. V.J. laughed and rolled in hysterics as Gideon's car hit the drawing of a tree and flipped over, complete with Gideon's dramatic sound effects.

Charisse had to turn away. Her heart raced. With eyes closed, she took a steadying breath. *V.J. didn't see his father die. Gideon's antics wouldn't hurt her son.*

Not the way they cut into her soul.

She concentrated on V.J.'s continued laughter and then Gideon's chuckle, but still, she could not face them.

"There's your mommy," Gideon said.

Another deep breath and Charisse turned.

V.J.'s laughter stopped and only a trace of his carefree happiness remained. "Mommy, do we have to go now?"

"In a few minutes."

"Judge Tabor?" He turned his attention to his new playmate.

Gideon stretched. "Yeah, Veej."

Charisse shook her head. He'd started calling V.J. by that name on Saturday. A fallback from his football days when the players gave each other nicknames, she guessed

"We have show-and-tell day at school. We can bring a person, a place, or a thing. Will you come tomorrow as my person?" V.J. picked up the cars.

Gid packed them away and lifted the sketchpad, tearing off the drawing. "Mind if I keep it here for your next visit?" He snatched tape from the roller on this desk and stuck the drawing on his wall with his diplomas and certificates.

She wished with all her heart he hadn't pasted it there where she would see it each day.

"I can come back?" V.J. spun toward Charisse.

She wrenched her gaze from the drawing and shrugged.

"Whenever you want, but next time no missing school, okay?" Gid moved to the personal calendar he kept and flipped a few pages. "So what time tomorrow?"

"We have show-and-tell at ten thirty and then go to lunch. Show-and-tell people can stay and have lunch if they wanna. Do you wanna?"

Gideon hesitated, studying the page in front of him. He flipped it over and back. Charisse held her breath. He had a special hearing. She'd scheduled it for him. V.J. was in for another dose of disappointment.

Gideon looked up. "I'm all yours, Veej."

V.J. ran to her and threw his arms around her hips. "Mommy, he can do show-and-tell."

"Thank you," Charisse mouthed her gratitude.

Gideon nodded and picked up his phone. "Marlene, I need you to reschedule the eleven o'clock hearing on tomorrow's calendar. Just tell them something very important has come up and give them my apology. Thanks."

Chapter Six

Charisse didn't need a mirror to know her face was beet red. Sweat dripped from every pore. She shouldn't have mown the lawn, but the neighbor met her at her car door when she and V.J. pulled into the garage. Mrs. Dunlap demanded something be done, or she would report Charisse to the city.

Dusk fell before Charisse finished with the heavy labor, and her migraine had fully bloomed. She entered the house through the garage, and V.J. handed her the phone. "Mrs. Carlyle." His shoulders slumped forward, and his lips puckered at the mention of his teacher's name.

Charisse lifted his chin with her finger and winked before taking the phone. "Yes, Mrs. Carlyle. How may I help you?"

V.J. trudged to the kitchen sink.

"Mrs. Wellman, I hope I haven't called at a bad time."

She had, but Charisse wouldn't tell her so. "You're fine."

"I wanted to talk to you about V.J.'s lack of enthusiasm concerning his school work. He seems listless, often not completing his class assignments. I understand you and V.J. are still in mourning over your husband."

"We miss him, yes." Charisse wiped her hand across

her forehead and looked there at the dirt and grass her action removed from her face. No wonder she had a migraine.

"I'm concerned about V.J."

Charisse moved into the dining room. Dizzy, she grabbed for the back of a chair. In her other hand, she gripped the telephone.

"I've seen this before with students who lose a parent, but it seems V.J. is moving slower than normal through the grieving process for a child his age."

V.J. brought her a glass of water, and Charisse sank into the chair. "Thank you, baby," she whispered.

He made his way upstairs, ducking down to watch her through the openings in the banister as he climbed. When he disappeared from view, Charisse stared into her living room at the picture on the shelf.

Vance.

If she could imagine him here, listening to her on the phone, she could keep her temper from showing and possibly keep herself from passing out. She gulped the water.

"Mrs. Wellman, perhaps you don't understand the implication of V.J.'s extended mourning."

Charisse swallowed. "I live with it every day, Mrs. Carlyle. We're working our way through this the best we can."

"I've spoken with his first grade teacher. She says she sees no change in him, and his father died over a year ago."

"I know when my husband died." Charisse squeezed her eyes shut. As fate would have it, she'd watched the life ebb from Vance.

"We feel both of you need grief counseling. A psychiatrist will help you deal with your son's issues."

Charisse shook her head, though the teacher couldn't see. "No."

"No?" The puzzled voice challenged. "You don't feel it would benefit your son to speak with someone who might help him? The school psychologist believes a psychiatrist can prescribe medication to offer the relief V.J. needs to see the reality of things. The cloud of sadness can be lifted, and he can move on. I know this is a lot to take in. I'd like to schedule a meeting. You could talk—"

"With respect to your professionals, I will not have my child speak with an individual who works in a system that maintains a cure-all for every ailment comes in the form of a pill." That solution had gotten Charisse's mother nowhere. She continued to take the drugs more than twenty years after Charisse's father walked out on them, never coping with his abandonment. "I'm sorry, Mrs. Carlyle. In situations like this, medication only covers the pain. A person isn't able to deal with his problems."

Charisse covered her eyes with her hand, shutting out the light. She could have sworn she'd clearly spelled out her stance on more than one occasion. "My son lost his father. Grief takes its own pace in each of our lives. Some get up and move on. Some deal with it a little slower. They release it a little at a time, and I will not have anyone …" Her voice shook. "I will not allow anyone to speak to V.J. and ask him to cover up his emotions because a group of teachers or a school psychologist believe they know more about my child than God or me."

"We are not implying we know more about your child than you. We're merely offering you the resources available to help V.J." Mrs. Carlyle softened her voice. "Your son needs help with his lack of interest, this lingering sadness."

"And you think a professional who doesn't know my boy, someone who really doesn't care about V.J. or the things he shared with his dad, you think that person can make him laugh and smile and go on with life? Where my son is concerned, I'm the professional, Mrs. Carlyle, not you or anyone else. If or when I decide V.J. needs counseling, we'll do so through our church, and we'll do it without drugs. Thank you, but I don't need a meeting with anyone at the school."

"It's possible that without help V.J. will continue to lack energy and interest in life around him. If you don't take appropriate steps now—"

"I have been taking appropriate steps." Charisse sighed. "Because they don't meet with the school's timetable of idealistic nonsense, it does not mean I'm being negligent. I'm trying to let my son's grief run its course. I love him very much. I guess now you're going to say I'm an unfit mother." Charisse stood and staggered into the living room. She picked up the photo of Vance and took a quivering breath. "I'm capable of taking care of V.J's needs, and if you interfere with my parenting one more time, we'll take this matter to the school board. Do you understand me?"

"Mrs. Wellman, I can see we'll get no further with

this conversation."

"Good night, Mrs. Carlyle."

"Good night, Mrs. Wellman."

Charisse pushed the end button, staring at it for a long moment. She raised the phone above her head with every intention of throwing it against the wall. Instead, she tossed it on the couch. "Vance!" she screamed her husband's name. "Why? Why did you leave us? Couldn't you just pass someone stranded on the highway for once in your life?" She threw the picture onto the floor. The glass shattered around her. "I hate you. I hate you. I hate you." She slid to the floor, feeling the glass dig into her jeans.

She didn't care.

"I hate you," she whispered the words one more time. "Because I love you so much, and V.J. loves you so much."

"Why, God? Why?" She cried out and then sobbed into her hands. "Vance said You entrusted us to him. Why, then, would You take him away? Show me. Just give me a little understanding."

She sat for some time among the shards of glass, her head pounding, her body drained of energy.

The Citrus Restaurant offered Gideon the relaxation he needed as he waited for his guest to arrive. The gentle clank of dishes, the soft candlelight on the tabletop, and the muted conversations from neighboring tables all worked to lessen the burdens of the day. He lifted and lowered his shoulders to relieve the tension in his neck. His guest tonight would be much better company than the one he'd dined with two nights before.

"Bad day?" Deacon Foster slipped into the seat on the other side of the booth.

"Tough ruling. I didn't make one party very happy."

"Not your job, boy."

The auburn-haired waitress waltzed over to them, the one he suspected despised Delilah James. "Judge Foster." She smiled. "How are you tonight?"

"Doin' fine, little lady. You can just bring me my usual with a sweet tea."

"For you?" She turned her blue eyes to Gideon, and her smile vanished. Guess he was guilty by his association with Delilah.

"My usual." He already had his tea.

She turned on her heels, and Gideon drew back as her long braid flew toward him. Deacon raised his brows but said nothing.

"The last time that girl waited on me Delilah showed up. We ended up dining together, and before the evening ended, Dee created a scene about an overcooked steak. Had to be overcooked, she said, because to complain about an undercooked steak means they can bring it back to you with spit on it. According to Delilah, with an overcooked steak, you get a free meal because you're not going to wait for another one. I don't know why she cares. I always pay."

On Saturday evening, Delilah had been better behaved, but Gideon had a strong feeling the wait staff always drew straws to see who would deal with Dee when she entered. With Deacon sitting at the table with him, if she showed up tonight, she'd move on quickly.

Deacon shook his head. "Yer blind as a bat, boy."

"What?" Gideon demanded.

"You already know what. Delilah's a problem."

Gideon sat back and stared into the candlelight. "Well, you'll be happy to know I did set some things straight with her over the weekend."

"Yet you entertained her in your office after lunch today. You may have set the matter straight as far as you're concerned, but that woman isn't going to be satisfied with friendship. Did you even realize she piled a ton of work on Charisse and left the poor girl scramblin'? Any other gal who gets near you is a threat so far as Delilah is concerned. She wants more than you're willin' to give. How many of your other girlfriends treat you the way she does?"

"She's not my girlfriend. Never has been." Gideon rubbed his neck. His muscles ached under his touch. Not what usually happened when he joined Deacon for a meal.

Deacon shook his head. "Well, how many of your old girlfriends call you by that ridiculous name she uses?"

"She's only a friend."

"Listen to me, Young Gideon, please. Women like Delilah can't be friends with a man like you." Deacon leaned back as the waitress returned with a basket of bread. He thanked her and set about cutting a piece and slathering it with butter.

"And apparently not with a man like you either." Gideon grinned before drinking his tea. He sliced the bread and bit into it. Even without butter, the flavor burst into his mouth. "Hmm, good."

"Okay, let's change the subject from one woman I never care to discuss to another who is a delight to this old man. What in the world did you do today to make Charisse so angry?"

The bread lodged in Gideon's throat. He coughed, swallowed some tea, and coughed some more. "Angry? What do you mean?"

"I sure got the idea if she had so much as a nail file, she'd have filleted and served you up with a helpin' of grits and hush puppies. Shame on you, too. Anyone could see the girl wasn't feelin' well."

The bread finally left Gideon's windpipe. He pushed his plate away. The waitress offered both men more tea, and they accepted.

Gideon had chastised Charisse over the missing research, work he never asked her to do. When she'd left the completed research for him, he assumed her attitude stemmed from her worry over her son, not from his earlier behavior.

"Seems to me somebody ought to make amends, and right quick, before she deems you too much a hassle to stick around." Deacon eyed him. "That happens, Zelma will make you wish you were never born."

Gideon reached into his back pocket and pulled out his cell phone. He checked its database and punched the numbers he'd dialed the evening he'd hired her. Good thing he'd programmed her number into his phone.

"Hello." Charisse's muffled voice reached into Gideon's heart.

"How are you?" he asked, returning Deacon's glare.

"I'm fine."

But she wasn't. The hesitation in her voice gave it away.

"Charisse, I wanted to tell you how sorry I am for acting the way I did this morning."

Except for a sniffle, silence filled the line.

"Are you crying?" He wiped his mouth. "Charisse, what is it?"

Deacon leaned forward.

"It's—I don't know what to do, Gid."

Why did a woman's tears always make him feel inadequate, especially ones he might have caused? Gideon pulled the phone away from his ear, and Deacon swatted the air with his hand in a silent admonition to continue listening.

"… you, the job, V.J.'s teacher, and I'm not well."

"You wait there." Gideon ended the call and tried to catch the eye of the waitress. "Excuse me, miss."

His undeserved nemesis glared at him from another table. A waiter came to him instead. "Yes, sir."

"If it's not too late, please cancel my order."

"I'll take care of it, sir."

The man left them, and Gideon panned through his phone searching for an Internet white-pages directory.

"What's wrong with that little gal?" Deacon asked.

"She needs someone with her. I don't know her address."

Deacon pulled out his own device and scrolled through his screen. "She invited me to dinner next Sunday, gave me her address so I'd have it for the occasion." He held up his phone, and a second later,

Gideon's buzzed with a received message.

"Thanks." He tossed money for both their meals on the table. "Gotta go." Running out the door, he nearly collided with a lady selling roses. Wallet already in his hand, he rifled through the bills. He finally gave up and handed her a hundred. "Give me all I can have for this."

The weathered old woman stared at the bill and then at him. "Take all you can carry, mister."

Gideon scooped nearly three-dozen yellow roses in his arms and headed toward his car, sending a silent prayer of thanksgiving to God for the invention of GPS.

Chapter Seven

"It's him, Mommy." V.J. burst into Charisse's bedroom. She sat up with a sleep-drugged moan as he tugged at her bathrobe. "I checked before I opened the door. I promise. Hurry. He wants to see you."

She wiped her eyes, trying to figure out what was going on. After making it up the stairs, she'd managed to take a shower. Then she'd draped her robe around her and had fallen asleep on the bed covers. Tears still dampened her face.

In his excitement, V.J. didn't seem to notice.

"What?" Charisse swung her legs over the side of the bed. The room tilted, and she closed her eyes.

"Judge Tabor. He's here. He asked me to get a couple of Band-Aids."

"Band-Aids?" She opened her eyes.

"The thorns cut his hands and his arm."

"Thorns?" She shook her throbbing head. Was she dreaming? Why would Gideon Tabor have cuts on his arms from thorns? Why would he be in her home?

Had she spoken to him on the phone or had that been a dream?

"Come see, Mommy." V.J. pulled on her arm.

Charisse pushed to her feet and caught a glimpse of herself in her dresser mirror. Puffy eyes stared back at her, and the tattered bathrobe—it had to go. Her blonde strands hung wet and straight down her back, and her face held blotches of redness. "The Band-Aids are in your bathroom drawer. I'll be right down." With Gideon Tabor around, she might have to stock an emergency kit—when she could afford one.

"Hurry before he leaves." V.J.'s padded Spiderman slippers thumped across the carpet.

She stumbled into her closet, feeling like a marathon runner in the last mile of the race when all she'd done was mow the lawn. She had to sit down in order to slip on her jeans and top.

She managed to get from her closet to her bathroom, close the door, and run a wet cloth over the telltale signs of distress. That's all that could be done. Nothing would help the circles under her eyes, and the evidence of her crying would diminish only with time.

"Mommy," V.J. called, his voice filled with little-boy eagerness. "He's waiting. Hurry, Mommy."

"He misses a man in the house so much, Lord. Just one more proof that I'm not enough." She could never be enough. He needed his father. She again caught sight of herself in the mirror and lowered her head.

She needed his father.

Charisse made her way down the stairs. V.J. sat on the couch helping Gideon place a bandage over a cut on his arm.

Charisse paused at the foot of the stairs. "What do we have here?"

Gideon stood and reached for the pile of roses he'd apparently abandoned on the table. "Ouch."

Charisse winced at the blood on the back of his hand.

"Don't worry, Judge Tabor. I have more Band-Aids."

"Thank you, Veej." Gideon stumbled forward, tripping on the leg of the coffee table. She hadn't cleaned up the broken glass, and it crunched under his shoes. "Charisse, I acted like a dope this morning. I'm sorry." He handed the fragrant bundle to her.

She wanted to laugh, but the events of the day wouldn't leave her alone. Tears once again rolled down her cheeks. She took the flowers with caution. Her anger with him seemed so far removed from the rest of the horrible day.

"Charisse?" He stood in front of her. "Please forgive me."

Unable to face Gideon or her son, she turned and walked toward the kitchen. Dizziness rocked her as she passed the dining room table. She braced herself against it before making her way into the other room. The large vase she wanted was within reach in her nearly empty pantry. She took the container with her to the sink and filled it with water. Arranging the roses helped her hide her tears and the weakness threatening to make her fall to her knees.

"Come here."

Charisse closed her eyes, letting the caring tone of Gideon's words wash over her. She cried harder, leaning over the sink as sobs wracked her aching body. The smell of roses made her stomach roll.

"If I did this to you, I deserve a thousand daggers." His warm hands rested on her shoulders.

Against her will, she turned into his embrace. She laid her head against his broad chest. His heart beat quickened, and she allowed it to lull her out of her tears.

"Tell me about it." His deep voice reverberated in her ears. She clung to him, and he tightened his embrace. "You can talk to me." His warm breath brushed against her hair.

How long had it been since she'd felt a man's touch?

Charisse tensed. Not this man. Never this man. That dream had passed. He'd betrayed her.

"V.J." She pulled out of Gideon's touch and stepped around him.

V.J. stood in the doorway.

"Sweetie, it's past your bedtime."

"Aw, Mommy." He whined.

Gideon led Charisse to the table in the nook. He pulled out a chair and helped her to sit. "Hey, Veej, let's go upstairs, and I'll tuck you in. We need to discuss strategy for tomorrow's performance."

Her little boy's face lit up.

"Is that okay?" Gideon turned to her.

How could she deny her son this small bit of happiness? She nodded.

"I'll be back, and we'll finish our talk."

Charisse's energy swirled away like water released to a drain. She laid her head in her arms and closed her eyes, listening to V.J. ramble on about his show-and-tell while Gideon trailed behind him up the steps.

Gideon tucked the covers around V.J. and sat beside him on the bed. "You're an awesome kid. Do you know that?"

"I am?" V.J. brought a stuffed dog closer to him, snuggling it in his arms.

"Yeah, you are. What's the doggie's name?"

"Rolf." V.J. barked the moniker.

Gideon laughed at the little boy's ingenuity. "So, what should I talk about tomorrow?"

"You can tell them you're a judge, and you judge people."

Simple. Easy. Straightforward. "Okay, I'll do that."

"Judge Tabor?"

"I'll check with your mother, but I don't mind if you call me Gideon or Gid if she doesn't."

"The mean lady who came into your office today called you *Giddy*." V.J. giggled.

"But you're not going to call me that, are you?"

"No, sir." V.J. sobered and brought his arms on top of the covers. "Have you ever asked a mommy to divide her kid in half and give half of him to another mommy?"

Gideon straightened. "What?"

"Like King Solomon in the Bible. The two ladies were fighting over a little boy because one of them had a son who died. They both told King Solomon the alive boy was theirs. Mommy said King Solomon acted as a wise judge. When he told them that's what they had to do, the real mommy told the king the other lady could have her son because she didn't want him to die."

The kid knew more Bible than he did. "No. I don't think that would work nowadays." Not unless every mother was like this kid's mom. How had Charisse hid her sickness from V.J.? Or had she? Gideon cast a worried glance toward the door.

The feel of the small hand over his brought a lump to Gideon's throat. He'd never experienced such a sweet, innocent touch.

"Would you say what you said about Mommy to the class tomorrow?" V.J. asked.

"What did I say?"

"Today you said she's your *bestest* worker. My teacher called tonight, and Mommy got upset. I think Mrs. Carlyle called her a bad mom."

"Why would anyone say that?" His astonishment came out as an inappropriate question to a hurting little boy.

V.J. shrugged. "Maybe because Mommy left me at school so long."

Gideon touched V.J.'s nose with the tip of his finger and stood. "I'll be sure and tell them about your mommy. I'm afraid, Veej, Mommy's delay in getting to you was my fault."

V.J. reached out to Gideon.

Not knowing what the boy wanted, Gideon shrugged his confusion.

"A hug, Judge Tabor. You hugged Mommy to make her feel better. I want to make you feel better."

Gideon wrapped his arms around the little boy. "Good night, Veej, and good night to you, too, Rolf."

On his way out of the room, Gideon turned off the light. He paused and stared back into the darkness, lit only by a small nightlight on the other side of the room. How could the child accept him so easily?

Three words could only describe what he felt. *Shock and awe.* He'd heard that term used on the news before. The effect of mortars and bombs could never compare with the love and trust in that kid's eyes.

"'Night, Judge Tabor." V.J. turned on side, pulling Rolf with him and holding the stuffed animal tight.

"'Night, Veej. See you tomorrow."

"Okey dokey."

Charisse had drifted to sleep, and Gideon's return to the dining room table startled her. He pulled out a chair and sat next to her.

"I'm worried about you." He reached for her hand and held it. "You're shaking."

She looked up. "I'll be fine. I overdid it today. That's all."

"I'm really sorry, Charisse. I got wrapped up in my selfish needs, and I didn't stop to think you would never let a deadline pass without a good reason."

She couldn't look up at him. "I'm not perfect, Judge Tabor." She grabbed a napkin from the holder on the table, sniffled, and swiped it under her nose.

"What happened to Gid? We agreed to it on Saturday. I don't understand this formality between us."

She stared at the paper in her hand. "You're my boss. We need to keep it formal." She needed the distance. "I'm sorry."

He pressed his warm palm against her cheek, and she looked up into his green eyes.

"You should apologize every time you insist on calling me Judge Tabor. Now, let's start over. Tell me what's wrong besides my acting like a moron."

"Nothing."

"Okay, let's start with what I do know. Veej seems to believe his teacher said you were a bad mother."

Charisse opened her mouth and snapped it shut.

"Yes, he overheard."

She would not cry in front of him. Not again. The time for dreams had passed. She had a son to think about. "V.J.—Vance's death hit him hard, Gid, and I don't know how to help him."

"I think you're denying the obvious."

She blinked.

"Your husband's death has knocked the wind out of both of you, but unlike the aftermath of our collision on Saturday, it's not that simple to catch your breath and recover."

He had no way of knowing that his choice of words slashed her like a razor. She needed to remember he didn't mean to hurt her. Yet he was right. She lowered her head, nodding.

"What set off this teacher?"

"The school ..." The battle with her emotions ended in her defeat. Tears spilled over and fell down her face. "I want my son back, and I can't reach him. They expect me to work miracles with him. How do I reach into his little heart and make everything better? They want him to see a psychiatrist."

"That's ridiculous. He appears sad on occasion, but he needs time. You need time."

"I know." She pounded her fist onto the table. "But they'll get him to talk to some well-meaning drug pusher who'll insist he take medication to hide the symptoms. They won't let him deal with it. It took me years to get over childhood grief." She looked up into his compassion-filled eyes. She'd had this discussion with him before. Would this time go any better than it had in high school?

He smiled and brushed back her hair. His palm was warm as he cupped her cheek, and mixed with the cool touch of wet strands against her face, the sensation was welcoming.

"I remember your grief." He tilted his head. "And I'm sure you remember mine."

She nodded.

"So, they expect miracles to happen, and if not, they'll take matters into their own hands?" He drew away, leaving only the cold.

"You're the one working miracles with him. Thank you for Saturday, for today, and for agreeing to go with him tomorrow. It means a lot. I've had to disappoint him too much lately and telling him I couldn't go to show-and-tell—"

"Why would you say that?"

"I've been working for you less than two months, and I didn't want to ask for time off." She wiped her tears with the back of her hand.

"You know, I haven't seen you in years, but what is it about our past that makes you believe I've become an ogre who won't give you two hours off to attend a school activity?"

Charisse stared up into his questioning face, and the

angry retort died in her thoughts like a doused ember. He was so sincere, so completely oblivious to the pain he'd caused her.

"I'm some piece of work, huh?" He looked away and back to her. "Don't answer that. I know I have my moments. God's working on me. Give me time. I'll stop my tantrums."

"It's not your fault. I took the job. I intend to do my best."

"Putting me, a job, or anything before your son isn't right. I might be new in my relationship with Christ, but I think God would want Veej to take priority, too."

"But when a woman becomes both mother and father and the job is what keeps the child safe and warm at night, sometimes you have to make tough decisions. Wait until you have a child. You'll understand." Charisse stared at the shine on the table. Her blotchy face and red eyes stared back at her.

"I've always wanted seven or eight."

The number had decreased. He used to want ten or twelve—all boys—a baseball team or two basketball teams, he used to say—with two or three to spare.

"Why haven't you married?" she asked.

Gideon leaned back. "I'll tell you what. You answer one question for me, and I'll answer a dozen for you."

What could he want to know that was so important? She waited.

"Why are you so sick right now?"

Of all the questions he could have asked this was the least harmful. "A migraine. Some heavy work took a lot out of me today."

"Work as in what I asked you to do or the load Delilah placed on you?"

"No. No." She shook her head. She couldn't have him believe her job was detrimental to her health. "I can do work like that all day long."

He smiled. "Okay, now that I have you where I want you, tell me what you did today that drained you this badly?"

"That's question number two. You have to play by the rules."

He narrowed his eyes and made a face at her the way he used to do when she insisted he work out a problem on his own. "Okay, ask away. A deal's a deal. A dozen questions. I'm ready."

"Just one unless your answer leads to another." Experience taught her to be very specific with him. "Why aren't you married?"

"I fell in love once upon a time with a fantastic girl."

His words dripped like a Chinese water torture. "Why aren't you together now?" Why did she care? Her mind told her Gideon's love life didn't matter. Her heart screamed that nothing else mattered.

"I'm sure you've seen guys like me before, goofs who pine after a girl like you, but never get up the nerve to ask you out. I've dated a few times, but no woman has ever come close."

"Gee, Gid, hurt a girl's feelings, will you? You knew me back then. Who'd pine after me?"

"You're kidding, right?" He studied her face. "You've always been beautiful. What about college? I'm sure you were the object of every man's affections. I bet you had them falling at your feet. Your husband was either a very lucky man, or he had to fight hard to win your affections."

Did he not remember her extra seventy-five pounds, and her absolute geeky persona? "If anyone fell at my feet back then, it happened because I knocked them down with my large rear as I walked through the halls."

In high school her only desire had been Gideon. No other boys mattered until she met Vance. At first, she'd been unable to believe that someone so handsome would look in her direction. Vance had stolen her heart because he'd accepted her—all of her—extra baggage and all.

Charisse tore at the napkin she had clenched in her fist. "Did you ever tell this girl how you felt?"

"Nope. As hard as it might be to believe, today wasn't the first time I acted like a jerk. I treated her badly after she'd been kind to me."

His story wasn't too hard to believe. He'd played the jerk at least three times—this morning, another time with another girl, and the day she tried to share Christ with him—but who was counting?

"I shouldn't tell you this, but I promised the Lord if he gave me a second chance with her, I'd ask her to marry me. Silly dream, I know."

Charisse pushed her chair back and stood. She had to stop the pain, put a bandage around her heart. How could she both desire this man and hold such deep resentment toward him at the same time? The fantasy would die soon enough. The knife of anger would kill it. "She's a lucky girl. That kind of love is rare." She squeezed the words out.

"I don't know." He stood and moved into the living room.

She managed to get to the arch between the kitchen and the dining room and leaned against the wall to watch him step over the glass.

Gideon picked up the picture of Vance from where it had remained on the floor. He stared at it for a long moment. "Didn't you have that rare kind of love with your husband?"

"Yes, I did. We loved each other very much."

"You met him in college?"

She nodded. "I guess you could say he swept me off my feet. I knew I loved him because he made me forget this idiot I loved who never showed any real interest in me in high school."

He smiled back. "I guess if the idiot asked you to marry him, you'd say no?"

"I don't know. I gave the guy four years of my life, and he never noticed."

"What a fool."

"You said it, not me." She swayed but caught herself.

Gideon placed the photo back onto the shelf. They both gazed at the picture.

"What kind of accident?" Gideon asked.

"A car."

Gideon turned from the picture to her. "Charisse, I'm sorry."

"And everything's gone downhill since then." Her legs wobbled beneath her.

She didn't realize he had moved toward her until his arms went around her and his chin rested on top of her wet hair. Once upon a time, she would have thrilled at his embrace. If he had loved her then, there'd be none of this pain.

"Mommy, you gonna come tell me good night?" V.J. called.

And without her love for Vance, she wouldn't have the most important part of her life.

"You're in no condition to climb those stairs," Gideon said.

"I tuck him in every night." She looked up at him. "Besides, my bedroom is up there."

Gideon pressed his lips together. The mischief climbed into his eyes before the smile lit his face. "All right, then." He lifted her in his arms.

"Gideon, put me down." She wiggled in his hold.

"I will. Give me a sec." He carried her up the steps and let her down outside V.J.'s room. "Tuck him in. I'll wait right here."

Charisse gave him her most insincere glare.

A deep laugh rumbled from him as Charisse stepped into her son's room. She held to the furniture to keep upright and then sat beside V.J. She tucked the covers around his little body. "Did you say your prayers?"

"I forgot." He started to pull free from the covers.

"Honey, tonight, I think God would understand if you stayed in bed."

V.J. folded his hands. "Dear God, thank You for my mommy and my daddy."

Charisse choked back the sob.

"Dear God, I pray for Mrs. Carlyle. She needs to know Mommy loves me, and she's a good mommy. And dear God, keep Judge Tabor and Cletus safe. They're a lot of fun. I love Judge Tabor. He's really nice to me. Amen."

Charisse forced a smile into place and lifted her gaze to her son. "I love you." She kissed his cheek. "Sweet dreams." She slid first to her knees and then pushed up with her hands.

"Mommy, did you get sick mowing the yard again?" He drew Rolf closer to him.

"Yeah, honey, I did, but I'll be okay tomorrow. You know it makes my head hurt and that makes Mommy a little shaky. That's all." Reaching for the furniture, she made it into the hallway.

Gideon stood with his arms crossed over his chest. Moist eyes belied his toughness. "You mowed the lawn this evening on top of everything else?"

"My neighbor complained." She put a finger to her lips to quiet him. "I'll be fine, and I won't do it again."

"You're right, you won't."

If she had the energy, she'd tell him what he could do with his protective attitude. She'd tell him she was only his law clerk not his wife. She'd tell him to leave and never come back. Besides, he'd always loved some other woman. She opened her mouth to ask him to lock the door on his way out. "Gid," she whispered. "I can't do this anymore. Vance is gone, and I don't know what to do or how to go on."

"Charisse, you can do this. You've got friends, and we're going to help."

She gave no response. He was not her friend—not any longer. But for some reason, she wanted him to be.

He slipped his arm around her waist and pointed one way and then the other. "I'll walk you to your door, milady, but then I must take my leave after you've safely tucked yourself in."

She led the way.

They reached her bedroom door. "Thank you, Gid." She took one shaky step at a time.

"Charisse?"

She turned when she reached the bed.

"Don't try to undress. Just get in bed, and if you're not able to make it to work, don't worry about the office. You did enough work for three people today."

"I have to get up tomorrow." She lay down and covered herself up. "I have a son who needs me, but thank you."

He flipped off her lights. "I'll lock up. Promise me you won't try to go downstairs." He stood in the doorway for a long second. "When I say my prayers tonight, I'll be thanking the Lord for whatever that little guy sees in me."

She turned her face into the pillow as the pounding on her stairs announced his gallop away. "Everything," she whispered. "He sees everything he lost regained in you."

He moved around downstairs for a long while, and she wondered what he was doing until she heard the clink of the glass as he apparently swept it into a dustpan. The lights filtering up from downstairs darkened. The front door creaked. "Charisse, one more thing," he called up to her.

"Yes?"

"Don't ever be afraid to tell me when I'm disagreeable."

She smiled in the darkness. "You weren't disagreeable."

"Oh?"

"You were a real *idiot*."

Gideon's laughter followed him outside.

FAY LAMB

Chapter Eight

Charisse reached for the office coffeemaker and poured her third cup of the day. Holding three sugar packets, she ripped the tops and poured them into her mug. The clock read ten, but someone must have played a cruel joke and turned it back an hour or two.

She yawned. She hadn't slept well with Gideon Tabor trouncing through her dreams—again—but at least her headache was gone.

"Hey, are you ready?" Gideon grasped the top of the doorframe and leaned into the break room. His boyish action fed the emotions within her she thought long dormant.

She once reserved those feelings for her husband, and Gideon should be the last man to awaken them in her. She turned away from him. "For what?" She stirred her coffee.

He moved in front of her and tapped his watch. "Veej, show-and-tell, lunch. How'd you forget?"

"Judge Tabor—"

He shook his head.

"Gideon, I can't go."

"Nothing I gave you is urgent."

"I wish I could." She walked down the hall and into her office.

Gideon followed and stood on the other side of her

desk as she pulled out her next project. He reached for the file with the note written in red, each word underlined three times. *I NEED THIS BY NOON TODAY, JUDGE JAMES.*

He held it up. "When did she give this to you?"

"This morning." She reached for the folder.

He pulled it from her grasp and headed out the door. "De– Li–Lah!"

In less than a minute, he returned to her doorway. "Let's go. For future reference, Judge James is to clear any request for work through me. Even clearer, if I don't give it to you, you don't work on it. Okay?"

Who was she to argue with him? She picked up her purse and followed his long stride down the hall. He slowed his pace and pulled at her shirtsleeve like a little boy wanting to know the answer to a very important question. "You feeling okay?"

"Much better. Thank you."

He pushed the elevator's button. The door opened, and she stepped in beside him. Gideon pushed the button for the lobby as Delilah glared at them from the hallway. He waved and smiled. "Better stay about a hundred yards away from Dee at all times, Charisse." Gideon laughed as the elevator door slid shut.

"So, you've successfully made an enemy out of her for me—something I've tried to avoid."

"I read the story of Samson this morning. Her name couldn't be more appropriate, don't you think?"

Charisse raised her brows. "Is she a temptation to you, Gid?"

"No," he offered the quick retort. "That's not what I

meant." He shuddered as if the thought frightened him.

"She doesn't know the Lord, does she?"

Gideon grew somber. "No, and that's why I try to remain friends with her, hoping someday she'll listen."

Sadness for Delilah cloaked Charisse, but she brushed it off. Delilah would feed on her empathy, twist it, and use it for destruction.

The elevator stopped with a thud, and she followed Gideon to the parking garage. Silence filled the space between them until he opened his passenger door for her. He ran around to get in and then drove his sporty BMW out into the beautiful day.

"I remember when this girl tried to talk to me about a relationship with Christ, and I shut her out." He looked at her as if he expected her to say something. When she didn't answer, he continued. "I didn't want anything to do with it, but when Deacon introduced me to Jesus, I fell on my knees and cried like a baby. I felt free of emotions and pain I carried for years."

Praise God from Whom all blessings flow.

"Charisse, I should have told you a long time ago how sorry I was for my reaction to the gift you tried to hand me that night."

"The gift wasn't mine, Gideon." She stared out the window. "You didn't deny me. You denied Christ."

He remained silent.

"Maybe I should have picked a better time." She reached across and touched his arm. "Your dad had died, and well, we'd just done something highly unusual."

"And cathartic." He smiled. "I have a feeling what you shared with me about your father very few people in your life know. I went from comforting you to scoffing at you."

"Don't let it bother you." She withdrew her touch.

"I will never forget. You cared enough to soothe my grief by telling me about the Lord and his love for me. And I mocked you. The hurt expression on your face haunts me even today."

Charisse swallowed back her tears and focused her attention on the passing scenery of downtown Orlando. If she told him her hurt no longer came from what he'd done so long ago, but from what he'd done within the last year, would it make her burden any less? Would he understand?

She wasn't about to take that chance. "Judge Foster cares for you very much."

"He likes you as well. I heard a rumor you've invited him to dinner. That's nice, Charisse, real nice. Since his wife died, he spends a lot of time by himself. As a bachelor, I know how lonely that can be."

Charisse took a deep breath. On Saturday, Gideon had asked her and V.J. to join him for dinner. She hadn't realized he was lonely. "Why don't you join us?"

If only she could cut out her tongue. Why was she continually bent on facing him? The more time she spent with Gideon, the more she wanted to be with him. And that just wouldn't do.

"Are you sure?"

"V.J. would be thrilled." Her tongue took control, leaving her brain out of the equation.

"Tell me when, and I'll be there."

"This Sunday at two o'clock was the best time for

Judge Foster."

He turned his green eyes upon her. "Mind if I attend your church on Sunday?"

Charisse gave him her full attention. "I didn't realize you were still looking for a place to worship."

"Yeah, I stuck it out with Deacon's church for a while, but even he's encouraging me to find a younger congregation."

"Did you ever speak to Judge James about Christ?"

Gideon chuckled, nodding his head. "I hope someday she remembers my face as vividly as I remember your wounded expression."

Charisse squirmed. The warmth rose on her cheeks. He realized he'd hurt her the first time. She wrapped her heart around his apology.

"But there's something else. You're putting a wall up between us, and I can't understand why."

"I'm a single mother now. A lot has happened since you knew me. I'm a different person. That's all."

Lying lips are abomination to the Lord. But they that deal truly are His delight. Drat her childhood scripture memorization. God used it often to convict her.

Still, she clamped her mouth shut.

He swung the car into the parking lot of the school, jumped out, and ran around to open her door.

Gideon held his hand out and helped her from the car. "Charisse, with your permission, I'd like to spend more time with Veej, see if I can help him through his grief. I was older, and I think I bounced back quicker than the little guy, but I can relate to what he's going through."

Her breath caught in her throat. Gideon's friendship

with her son was both an answer to prayer and her worst nightmare all rolled into one tight ball. That ball threatened to unravel if she ever told Gideon Tabor what she really thought of him. "Thank you," she managed to say.

Trouble was, her mind and heart warred with one another. One moment she'd daydream of being entertained by his boyish charm for the rest of her life, and in the next, she'd roll a bazooka into the fantasy and blow it apart. She'd never get involved with *Judge* Gideon Tabor. He might have boyish charm, but he'd made a terrible mistake, one that cost her so much, and she couldn't let that go.

Then there was V.J.

Gideon, with that same boyish charm, pulled V.J. from his grief. How could she deny her little boy the companionship of this man who so readily agreed to attend show-and-tell, changed his calendar to make it happen, and allowed her to tag along when she should have been working?

V.J. never had to know the truth. But it didn't mean she had to let Gideon into her heart. No. That would never happen.

Gideon strolled the hallway with Charisse by his side. Outside the classroom, he perused the artwork on the walls until he spotted the picture with the bold "V.J." signed in the corner. He laughed.

Charisse poked him in the ribs. "You'll get us kicked

out of here."

He leaned toward her. "I wonder what Mrs. Carlyle thought of this picture," he whispered.

Charisse studied the drawing of a man and woman falling to the ground with a dog and a boy watching. She shook her head. "I can't imagine."

Gideon knocked and a middle-aged woman with streaks of gray in her otherwise blonde hair, opened the classroom door. "Gideon Tabor," he introduced. "The office told us it was okay to arrive early. I'm here for V.J."

"Please come in. I'm Mrs. Carlyle." The teacher offered a smile.

Gideon motioned for Charisse to stay put before he stepped inside.

V.J. waved, his hands high in the air, his body rising off the chair. "Judge Tabor, come sit here by me. I saved a desk just for you."

Gideon held the door open, and Charisse ducked inside.

"Mommy," V.J. called. "You came."

"I suspect he wanted you here more than me," Gideon whispered.

Mrs. Carlyle looked at her watch. "We're about to start. We present alphabetically. Do you have time? We can reverse the order."

"Veej, what's your last name?" Gideon teased before turning back to the teacher. "We have as much time as you need. We'd love to see the other presentations, and Veej invited us for lunch."

"Please have a seat. Bobby, please move to the empty

desk to let Mrs. Wellman sit beside V.J."

Bobby complied, offering a bright smile. Charisse touched his nose as he stood to offer his seat. "Hi, ya."

"Hi, Mrs. Wellman." Bobby beamed.

Bobby obviously liked Charisse—and what was not to like?

Mrs. Carlyle asked by a show of hands which students intended to give a presentation. Gideon counted eight out of the twenty or so second graders and settled behind V.J. in an uncomfortable child's desk with attached chair. Charisse took the seat to the right of her son.

V.J. swung his legs up and back, up and back. The kid turned to look at Gideon, and a sweet smile touched the boy's lips. Gideon felt like a valuable trophy. With each presentation and each smile tossed to him by V.J., Gideon fidgeted a little more. He'd always wanted a house full of kids. If men had biological clocks, the seconds ticking by on Gideon's pounded like a gong.

He looked at Charisse. She leaned forward in her chair, listening as a girl in the front of the room shared a book of poetry she'd written and illustrated. "My daddy helped me put it together. We make poetry books and picture books," the little girl said.

Charisse lowered her eyes. Gideon could not look away from her. A single tear fell onto the desk and branded Gideon's heart. No matter what Charisse said, she still missed her absentee father. Deep down inside, the strong woman she'd become still held to her insecurities and sadness.

Then the truth hit him.

He loved the woman she'd become and this son who made her complete. Someday, if God allowed him, he'd slay the dragon of sorrow keeping both their hearts in bondage.

First, though, he had to discover the monster guarding the wall she'd built against him.

"We're next, Judge Tabor," V.J. whispered.

When the little girl finished, Gideon maneuvered out of the desk, lifting it with his body.

Charisse's light giggle was his reward. He winked, and her smile brightened his day.

V.J. escorted Gideon to the front. "I'm showing and telling about my mom's boss, Judge Tabor. Yesterday I went to work with my mom. Judge Tabor and I played in his office. He has big pads of paper. He can draw, and he has these cars. He says people use them to tell him about their accidents, but Judge Tabor says he likes to draw towns on the paper and drive the cars down them."

The child's simple view of him filled Gideon with wonder.

"But Judge Tabor doesn't just play. He has another office, with a big desk. A lady sits beside him, but he sits high, and she's down lower in a *littlier* chair. Judge Tabor's chair is huge, and he has a hammer. He says he doesn't use it that much because people behave in his room. Go ahead Judge Tabor." V.J. ran back to his seat, flashing his mother a bright smile.

V.J's intro had garnered the children's rapt attention.

"Well, let's see. What can I say after that introduction? Veej said it all. How many of you have ever been in a courtroom?"

"I've never been in trouble," Bobby said from his substitute seat in the back of the room.

"You don't have to be a criminal to enter a courtroom. You can be a witness in a case, or you can come into a courtroom and just watch what goes on."

"Why do you have the hammer on your desk?" poetry girl asked.

"I use it when my law clerk gets unruly and thinks she knows more than me." He shared a smile with Charisse. "It's mainly for show, like a decoration on your mother or father's table. I do know some judges who use it if the courtroom gets loud, but I have a bailiff—a guard—to control the noise. My bailiff's name is Bill, and no one would get out of line with him."

"What does the lady do that sits beside you?" another little girl asked.

"She's my court clerk, and she takes notes of everything that happens in the courtroom. She writes up papers for my signature. In a trial, the court clerk makes people swear on the Bible before they tell their side of a story. She keeps all of the items that we call evidence in order, and she has a very important job." He glanced across the room, watching as the kids awaited his next comment. "She pinches me when I fall asleep."

The children laughed.

"What about V.J.'s mom?" Bobby spoke up again.

"Mrs. Wellman is my law clerk. I'd like to invite you to my office if Ms. Carlyle can arrange it. I'll show you around the courthouse. You'll be able to talk to Mrs. Wellman, and she can show you what she does."

At his desk, V.J. looked to his mother and back to

Gideon and mouthed, "Remember?"

Gideon smiled. "Mrs. Wellman is the best clerk I've ever had work for me."

V.J. sat tall before turning to his mom. "And she's the best mommy in the world, too, Mrs. Carlyle."

Charisse leaned against the elevator wall. "Gideon Tabor, I'm sure Mrs. Carlyle will never invite you back."

"Why?" He sipped the soda he'd insisted on getting before heading back to work.

She laughed. "A speed-eating contest, that's why. V.J.'s buddy, Bobby, nearly choked on his peas."

"Well, he won, didn't he? No pain. No gain."

"If V.J. had won, I'd have been mortified."

"Ah, come on, Charisse. He's a boy. Didn't you have a kid in your class who made everything fun?"

"Yeah." She laughed. "Gideon Tabor."

"And I wear that badge with pride. V.J. needs to be that kid. He's a natural. That little speech he gave about me, wow. He poured it right out without notes or anything."

Charisse touched her hand to her heart. Someone else saw in her son what she'd always seen.

"Speaking of V.J., did you see Mrs. Carlyle's face?"

"When?" she asked.

Gideon chuckled. "When he set me up for that little snub at his teacher. That kid of yours is a genius, pure genius." They walked out of the elevator and down the hall toward the office.

"What'd he do?" Charisse trailed a step behind.

"He asked me to tell the class what I thought of you as my clerk. I bet he was awake most of the night making sure he got the timing perfect for his little retort. That boy loves you."

Delilah walked toward them. "Well, I see you've returned from recess."

Gideon stopped. "Hey, Dee." He held out his arm preventing Charisse from moving in front of him.

Was she imagining it, or was Gideon acting as a shield against the other woman? Charisse looked over his shoulder at her nemesis.

Delilah ignored Gideon and instead waved a sheet of paper around him and toward Charisse. A sneer crossed her face. "You had a call from a member of your high school reunion committee. They've changed the meeting from Saturday to Friday."

Charisse reached for the paper, but Gideon retrieved it first. Charisse never lifted her gaze from the malicious turn of Delilah's lips. That woman was up to something.

Gideon handed Charisse the note. "The Magic are playing Friday. I planned to ask if I could take Veej. Need a babysitter?"

Charisse folded the message. "He'd love to go, Judge Tabor. Thank you."

"Can't find anyone your own age to play with, Giddy?" Delilah brushed close to him as she stepped past.

"Excuse me." Charisse walked into her office and sat at her desk. She opened the note. "Libby Overstreet, Astronaut High School Reunion Committee. Meeting changed from Saturday to Friday." Delilah had scribbled the phone number and made sure she signed the note. Nothing that would give Delilah anything to use against her.

"I've been looking forward to the reunion." Gideon joined her in her office.

"Really?" she teased. "Why in the world would you care? Inductions into high school athletic hall of fames happen all the time, don't they?"

"That's an honor, but that's not why. That girl I mentioned, the one I said I'd ask to marry if she was available. I heard she's attending." He brought his elbow into his body, palm up, fist clenched. "And she's single."

Charisse turned to her computer and blinked back tears. Why should she feel as if he'd just lost her best ex-friend? She was still angry with him, right?

He stepped closer. "You okay? You don't look well." He reached across her desk and touched her arm. "Charisse, are you still having the same trouble you had last night?"

"I need to talk to you about something." She looked up at him.

Delilah stopped in the doorway.

Charisse pulled from Gideon's touch. "Later. It's not important now."

Delilah walked on.

"Can you take it easy this afternoon, not be up and down?"

She nodded. "I'll do that, but I'm okay. Cross my heart."

His smile returned. "I have court in a few minutes." He walked out of her office.

"The research is on your desk," she called.

He turned in the hallway. "And I didn't have to act like an idiot to get it. Amazing."

Charisse forced the smile but allowed it to fall away as soon as he entered his office and closed the door. She lowered her head.

Hadn't she been missing the sympathy Vance always offered? If possible, Gideon's seemed almost as endearing. She took a quivering breath. He showed so much concern, yet her smoldering anger sometimes flamed into a raging fire. She'd run out of reasons to justify her actions.

Right now, she wasn't so sure she could maintain her ire with him. The point was moot, though. He was attending their class reunion to get reacquainted with an old love.

Crystal walked by, paused, and shook her head before continuing on.

Today had been Crystal's turn to man the reception desk at lunch. Probably hoping to gain some points with her boss, she'd allowed Delilah to talk to Libby. What could she hope to find?

Libby, bless her heart. Her friend trusted everyone, and why shouldn't she? Charisse never told her she worked for Gideon. When Libby couldn't reach her on her mobile phone, she probably called the courthouse operator and asked to speak with Charisse.

Charisse rubbed tired eyes. She couldn't blame Crystal or Delilah. She shouldn't be here. As soon as she heard the position was with Gideon, she should have walked out the door and never looked back. But where would she and V.J. be without this job? Things were a little better, but she was one paycheck away from her son living on the street with her.

Before Delilah had the chance to piece together the pictures, she'd have to tell Gideon the truth. Of course, she'd only tell him the particulars, and she'd try her best to leave out all the emotion: pain, anger, sorrow, and … love.

She shook her head. No. She didn't love Gideon. That would be betrayal to the man whose life Gideon had devalued with his ruling.

"My, my, Charisse Taylor, how you've changed." Delilah slithered into Charisse's office. "It's so hard to believe the description Giddy once gave of you."

How had Delilah learned her maiden name? Had Libby used it when she'd called? Charisse stood and looked past Delilah to Gideon's closed office door.

"He's on the phone," Delilah shared. "So tell me. How did a once homely girl manage to land a job with the old high school classmate?"

Once homely? Well, that was comforting. She was no longer ugly at least in Delilah's eyes. "I qualified for the position." Delilah's arrow found its mark, but Charisse refused to flinch.

"Charisse," Delilah shook her head, "I don't know why you'd want to work for a man who said such things about you."

"Judge James, I'm not having this conversation with you."

"The little hometown girl. Only he didn't say little. Obese, I believe. Yeah, something nicer than fat." Delilah narrowed her eyes and then widened them as if something had just occurred to her. "'An obese little stalker' is what he called you. Followed him around like a love-starved puppy, didn't you?"

Charisse moved to the door and held it open. "Excuse me, Judge James. I have work to do."

"Working for a boss who thinks so little of you." Delilah tsked. "Don't you have an ounce of pride?"

Charisse took a deep breath. "When you lose your husband to a hit and run driver, when the man apprehended for the crime—the man who killed the person you love most in this world is allowed to go free—when you have to make the decision between finishing school or feeding your son, between buying your son a birthday present or paying the light bill, you come back to me, and you tell me about pride and where it gets you. Now, get out of my office, and don't come back."

With great effort, Charisse closed the door without slamming it shut. She sat in her chair and stared at the screen.

Not only did Gideon think of her as a stalker. He told others she'd been fat.

He really was an idiot.

Chapter Nine

Charisse paced back and forth in her bedroom before going to her door. She tiptoed down the hallway to her son's bedroom door. V.J. sat with his back toward her, working on his homework at his desk. She'd almost changed her mind about allowing him to attend the game with Gideon, but V.J.'s excitement lightened her heart. No matter what Gideon said about her, V.J. didn't need to suffer.

His back to her, he hunkered over his work.

She knocked to let him know she was there. "You okay?"

He turned. "Mommy, Judge Tabor wanted me to call him when I'm done to tell him I can go. I need to hurry."

"You need to slow down and make sure your answers are correct. Do you need my help?" The deal was he had to finish his math assignment tonight to go to the game with Gideon on Friday, but that didn't mean she wouldn't help him with those pesky problems. In fact, she'd welcome the distraction.

"No, I'm okay."

She forced a smile and headed back to her room. The phone beckoned, and she picked it up, staring at the numbers before giving in and dialing. "Be home. Be home."

"Hello."

"Oh, Libby. I'm glad you're there."

"What is it? Is everything okay? V.J.'s okay?"

"He called me fat." Charisse lost the battle to remain calm. Instead, she cried.

"V.J.? You tell him Aunt Libby will paddle his behind."

"No, not V.J."

"Then who?" Libby asked. "I'll throttle them."

Charisse took a deep breath. "Gideon Tabor." His name came out in a rush of air.

"Gideon Tabor? Where in the world did you see him, and why would he blurt out something like that?"

"That's what he thought of me in high school. He called me obese."

"Well, which is it, Charisse? Did he say obese, or did he call you fat?"

Charisse pulled the phone away from her ear and stared before putting it back. "What difference does it make? Obese is fat."

"No. Now, obese is like—no, I'm sorry. That's plump. You're right. Obese is fat. What do you care what some overgrown jock thought of you in high school?"

Overgrown jock? How dare she say that about Gideon? He was kind and loving. When she was sick last night, he carried her up the stairs. She gasped then stomped her foot. Why couldn't she make up her mind about him?

She closed her eyes as the revelation fell upon her like rain washing away all the loneliness.

No matter what he'd said about her, he was the man she … she what?

Oh, you terrible, terrible traitor, Charisse.

"Are you there?" Libby asked.

"Yes, I'm here."

"So tell me why it matters what he thought of you?"

Charisse took a deep breath. Libby was the only person she could share with. "Because I've fallen in love with him all over again, and he's in love with someone else." Charisse hiccupped through her tears.

"Okay, but where did you see him?"

Oops. She hadn't been sharing with Libby lately. "Gideon is the judge—my judge. I work for him."

"Good name for a judge," Libby joked, and on any other day, Charisse would have laughed at such an unlikely statement from her friend. "So I can assume that since you're working with him, you've talked everything out with him, asked him why he did what he did, and you're okay with it?"

"Libby, I haven't told him about any of it. He already thinks of me as some loved-stared puppy who followed him all around high school." Thinking of it that way was less painful than saying he thought she'd stalked him. "That's embarrassing enough. Now, to tell him I took this job despite his error in judgment—he's sure to think I'm—I'm stalking him."

Yeah, that hurt.

"You have a point there. I mean about telling him, but I don't remember you as the one looking like the love-starved puppy."

"But I did. I was like his dog, Cletus, just waiting for him to pat my head." She sniffled and sat hard on the bed. "I'm sorry I didn't tell you. I haven't told anyone. I'm so ashamed."

"I knew something was up. You're too easy to read. I figured you'd tell me when you wanted. I am a little upset with you now that I know the truth. After all, a story like this could keep me entertained for days."

"I'm sorry if you're offended, but I'm hurting here. Gideon called me fat."

"Well, to be honest, you were a bit larger than you are today."

Charisse gasped at her friend's truthfulness before covering her mouth to stifle a giggle. Where had this Libby come from? "But he didn't have to tell everyone else what he thought of me."

"No, but he was a teenage boy. They're never too bright, you know. It's like God takes their brains away for a few years."

"No. You don't understand. He told Delilah."

"Just a plethora of Biblical names—Gideon, Delilah. And how do you know he told this Delilah? Is she the woman he loves? Delilah is supposed to destroy Samson's life, not Gideon's."

"Delilah used to be—oh, I don't know what they are to each other." Charisse stood and paced the room. "It hurts so much, Libby. I never thought it would. Not after Vance showed me I was more than my mirror image."

"I know Gideon never said anything like that to you when we were in high school."

"No." Charisse swiped the tears from her face. "He wouldn't."

"You're right. He wouldn't. And has he changed so much that he'd *really* describe you so rudely to someone today?"

Charisse hiccupped again. "No, Libby, that's just it. Despite everything, he's wonderful. Gideon would never say anything like that about anyone—ever. He's the same kind, sweet, wonderful man I've always known. If only you could see the way he is with V.J."

"He's met V.J.?"

Charisse bit her lip. If truths kept gushing out of her like water from a spigot, Gideon would know more than he should soon enough.

"Libby, I'm sorry I didn't tell you. I've struggled with my feelings. I've been angry, sad, and angry again, and now I don't know. He's just—"

"Kind and sweet and wonderful. I heard." Libby's voice held a hint of amusement. "So if Gideon didn't say these horrible things to you, who did?"

"Judge James told me."

Libby's exaggerated sigh rasped through the phone line. "And who is Judge James?"

"Delilah. Judge Delilah James."

"Charisse, my head is spinning."

"Delilah realized I'm the girl he told her about. She took your message today."

"Tell me, with the message I left, how did she put two and two together and come up with *fat, love-starved puppy stalker*, especially since we've established that the kind, sweet, wonderful Gideon Tabor would never say such things? You probably wear a size four now, but you sure didn't back then."

"Oh, shut up!" Charisse laughed despite herself. "And it would be a fat, love-starved stalker puppy. What do I do? I need the job, and now that I've found him—oh, goodness, Delilah's right. Maybe I decided to work for him because I am a stalker."

"Share what happened with him with the case. Ask him why? Maybe there's something you don't know about his decision." The voice of reason sounded through the line, but Charisse wanted nothing of it.

She'd started to ask him after Delilah presented the message, but her courage failed her for the remainder of the day. She shook her head as if Libby could see her. "I can't."

"Why?"

Charisse stopped in front of the mirror and stared at her slender shape. She looked into her own eyes, wet with tears. Her gaze swept to her wedding photo, to the man who showed her love wasn't something stirred by outward appearance. No, it was the connection of two people who enjoyed each other enough to want to be together for a lifetime.

Most of her memories of tutoring Gideon were happy ones. She enjoyed being with him. She swallowed—hard. Gideon had treated her the same way Vance had. Her weight hadn't mattered. Her status as a social nerd hadn't seemed to bother him either. "Whether I'm skinny or heavy, I'm still the same person."

"Gideon didn't look at your weight. I saw the way he stared at you in high school."

"I don't know."

"He has an expressive face, wouldn't you say?"

"Yes," Charisse agreed. And the most beautiful green eyes, and the sweetest dimples.

"Wears his little-boy heart on his sleeve?"

That was her Gid.

Her Gid.

She had to stop thinking like this.

"I'm so ashamed." Charisse wiped her tears with the back of her hand. "Vance …"

"Charisse, Vance would want you to be happy."

"Libby, it doesn't matter. Gideon let Vance's killer go free. How can I get past that?"

"From what I'm hearing from you tonight, I think you've gotten past it. Trouble is you keep doubling back to the point of beginning, holding on to something you need to release. Talk to him about it. Find out what he has to say, and then go after him. Girl, the guy was adorable. I'd try to steal him away from you if I thought I had a chance."

"Neither of us has a chance. Didn't you hear me? He's in love with someone else—someone from our class."

Libby laughed.

"It's not funny." Charisse tightened her grip on the phone.

"Oh, Charisse, love is so very blind, and I think you have the picture of your past relationship backward. You weren't the puppy dog."

"No, I was the big fat bulldog scampering at his heels while he was panting after some other girl."

"For goodness' sake. You're not ready to listen to me, so I'm going to stop talking."

"I never meant anything to him, and I never will." Charisse looked again to the picture of her husband.

Libby was right. Vance would want her to be happy—but with the man who let his killer go free?

"Charisse, have you prayed?" Libby cut into her thoughts.

"Uh-no," she admitted.

"Well, let's do that right now."

Charisse bowed her head. "I'm ready."

"Heavenly Father, we seek Your wisdom for Charisse. Hold her in Your arms, Lord, and cause her to feel, from You, the love she's missing so much from her husband. Guide her, Lord, in Your will as You are the head of her household. And Lord, shed light on the truth and close out the darkness in my friend's life. Father, help Charisse to forgive."

Charisse bit her lower lip. If she'd said the prayer, she'd have asked for retribution against those who wronged her in one moment and for Gideon's undying love and devotion in the next. Libby's prayer was perfect—except she wasn't ready to forgive. She wanted her husband's killer to come to justice. Then she'd be happy.

"I love you, Charisse," Libby said.

Charisse opened her eyes. "Thank you, Lib."

"Charisse?"

"Yeah."

"Don't judge the judge on the word of another judge, especially one named Delilah."

Charisse clicked off the phone. Who knew Libby could react with such humor, and who knew better about looking on the inside of people than everyone's friend? The seemingly naïve, sheltered Libby wasn't so sheltered or naïve after all.

"Was that Judge Tabor?" The expectant face of her seven-year-old stared at her from the doorway.

"Libby."

"Mommy, I wanted to tell her about Judge Tabor taking me to the basketball game." V.J.'s shoulders slumped, the papers in his hand dangling at his side.

"I'm sorry. You were working so hard on your homework. Did you get your problems done?"

V.J. held out the math equations. "Can I call him and tell him I can go?"

"Not until I look this assignment over, young man."

Gideon pulled the popcorn from his microwave. "Ouch, ouch, ouch, ouch." He batted the bag in the air several times until he reached the opposite counter. He pulled the sack apart, and jerked his hand back as the steam escaped. With care, he poured the contents into a bowl.

The doorbell rang, and Cletus ran, barking, to the door.

"Bad dog!" How intelligent was it to add his loud admonishment to the dog's racket? "You've gotten me in enough trouble with the condo association."

Cletus sat with his large tail sweeping back and forth across the tile floor. Gideon made his way through the room, popcorn in hand, and opened the door. "Delilah."

She stood before him dressed in black spandex from her thighs to her neck. Was cat woman attire in style again?

What a shame.

Cletus greeted Delilah with a nudge of his nose, and she patted his head before he retreated and stretched out by the couch.

"Giddy, I just finished at the gym, and thought I'd stop by."

Gideon pulled the door back and waved her inside. He held the bowl of buttered popcorn out for her.

"Now why would I want all that fat after my workout?"

He shrugged and sat on the couch. "If you want a diet drink, it'll have to be water. I don't believe in consuming anything that needs to be tested on animals before it's considered safe to digest."

"Always the charmer."

Funny thing for a snake to say. She needn't think he had missed the little scene between Charisse and her earlier in the day. Delilah was here to bury her fangs in him, but he'd play along, holding her at a distance like a reptile handler at the zoo. "So, what brings you by?"

"I'm a little worried that you hired Charisse. How much do you know about her life since you were in school? For instance, do you know what happened to her husband?" Delilah slithered beside him, sitting on the edge of the cushion.

Deacon gleefully told him he'd overheard Charisse finally giving Delilah an ear full. Truth was, Gideon feared if he ever got caught in an altercation between the two women, Charisse would walk out on him. He didn't know where the thought came from, but Charisse's leaving—that wouldn't do.

For a moment he considered asking Delilah about the exchange. He shook the ludicrous idea from his head. Delilah James could twist the wind if it gave her enough leverage. "I know all I need to know." He tossed a handful of popcorn into his mouth and chewed.

"Gid, I think you might want to reconsider her employment. We shared a clerk once. It'll cut expenses."

This was serious. She called him Gid. "We shared Crystal's limited expertise before I hired Stacey. You ran Stacey off, and now you've been using my clerk to fill the void caused by the inadequacies of yours."

"I did not run Stacey off. She got pregnant, remember?"

"Whatever story you want to believe," he baited.

"She stopped by with her little bundle of joy. As I recall, you cooed and awed like a fool over the little squirming thing."

"She chose to stay home after her maternity leave because of your antics. What's wrong? Charisse doesn't scare so easily?"

"There's something you should know about your clerk. She came undone on me, and she let something slip. This girl isn't just any widow—"

Gideon slammed the bowl down on the table, and the popcorn jettisoned into the air. Delilah startled. Kernels fell on the carpet, and Cletus rushed to clean up the mess, his tail wagging hard against Delilah.

She brushed Cletus away from her. Undaunted, the dog lunged to clean up the mess under the coffee table.

"Delilah, I love—I love Charisse's work. I'm happy

with her. I don't care what petty business you've dug up. I'm warning you now. You're stepping over the line."

"I care about you. She isn't what she seems. She may be dangerous."

Gideon laughed. "Charisse?"

"You know what I think?"

"I can't imagine." He sat back. This ought to be real good.

"You're being taken for a fool, and you're wearing a self-made blindfold to hide the truth from yourself. She may very well have a different reason for working for you, one you would never comprehend."

"Delilah, this can't be jealousy."

"I'm not jealous of her. I don't like her." She narrowed her eyes at him. "And now I know my instincts are correct."

"You didn't like Stacey either."

She lowered her eyes and remained quiet.

"What has Charisse Wellman ever done to you that would make you treat her this way? Do you know she actually asked after your welfare today? I got the feeling she really cares."

"Yeah, right." Delilah shook her head. "Why would someone like her care about someone like me?"

Gideon stared at her. He opened his mouth to speak but found no words.

"What?" Delilah asked. "Yeah, Giddy, I know I'm jaded and not easy to like. For me that's survival."

"Wow."

The word hung between them for a long moment. Gideon expected tears, but Delilah gave none.

"Is that why you treat me the way you do?" He raised a brow.

"I—I thought we were friends."

He nodded. "We are friends, but you make me work at it." He picked up the bowl of popcorn and walked into the kitchen. "You push my buttons at every turn. You like to see me squirm in front of people you treat badly, and you treat everyone badly, including me."

"Well," she huffed out the word.

"You treat Charisse even worse, but yet today, she asked about you. The woman has a mountain of cares, Dee, and she asked about you."

"She can take her concern and—"

Gideon raised his hand to stop her. He'd thought Charisse's compassion might break the hard heart. "Today or any day, if you'd like to talk to me about what's made you this way, I'll listen. After all, that's what friends should do. And by the way, I did hear about the unprofessionalism in our office today. Don't push Charisse to behave that way again, please."

She pinched her lips together and turned away from him, no longer holding her slender shoulders straight and proud. "I came here to tell you Charisse Wellman needs to go."

"If you do anything to jeopardize her position with me ..." He shook his head. "Charisse is my law clerk. I'm aware of everything I need to know about her."

"So you think, but what you don't know might cost you dearly."

"What are you getting at?"

"Forget it." She walked toward the door.

"All right, Dee. You win. Whatever it is you're dying to get out, go ahead and spill it." He braced himself for some horrible, twisted mistruth.

"Like you said, you're a veritable garden of knowledge. There's no need for me to say another word."

The ring of the phone jarred him.

"I'm expecting an important call. Hold on." Gideon retrieved the phone. "Hey, Veej."

"I got my homework done, Judge Tabor. Mommy says I can go with you."

"Good job. I've been waiting to hear from you. I'll see you Friday. And, Veej, I can't wait." He turned his back on Delilah. "Let me talk to your mom."

"Hi," Charisse answered.

"I wanted to check on you. You still feeling okay, not sick like last night?"

"I feel fine."

"You're sure?"

"You're hovering, Gid." Her words held a warning her voice did not convey. She liked him asking. He could tell.

"I'll stop hovering if you'll promise me you'll get to bed early tonight."

"I promise."

"Good girl." He smiled. "Now, remind me. What time is your reunion meeting on Friday?"

"I need to be there at seven."

"You'll have time to get something to eat before the meeting?"

"Gid, really. Yes, I'll take time to eat."

"Don't worry about feeding Veej. I'll pick him up at

six and ply him with some wholesome fast food and snacks at the game. We'll have time to buy him a hat or a shirt or something." He looked at Delilah, holding his finger up to ask her for one more minute—yet, he didn't want to let the call end. He again turned his back on Delilah.

"He's happy to be going with you. You don't need to buy him anything else." Charisse's voice was low and full of emotion. "Thank you so much for what you've done. He's been like his old self."

"He's my pal, Charisse. What else do friends do for each other?"

The door shut with an almost silent snap, and Gideon looked over his shoulder.

Delilah was gone.

"Charisse?" He closed his eyes.

"Yes?"

I love you. "Good night. Sweet dreams, okay?"

"Okay." She hung up.

Gideon looked down at Cletus. "How would you like a little boy to play with every day?"

"Woof." Cletus brushed Gideon with his paw.

"Woof is right." Gideon looked to the heavens.

Gideon stirred his coffee and leaned back in his chair. He closed his eyes. The lovely vision of Charisse Wellman sitting on a tree swing, a soft white dress caressing her shapely legs kept him awake all night.

He shook his head and opened his eyes. He had work

to do on this fine Friday morning. This evening, he looked forward to spending time with the little boy whose mother had captured his heart.

Who was he kidding?

Mother and son were precious to him.

"Mornin', Young Judge Gideon," Deacon entered with his usual greeting. He stopped in the doorway. "Sleepin' not an option? You look terrible."

"Close the door, will you?" Gideon motioned. "The noise is keeping me awake, and you never know who will walk in."

Deacon stepped back and pushed the door closed. He came back to stand in front of Gideon's desk. "When a man doesn't sleep, it means he's either sick or in love. Which is it?"

"Is everything ready for Saturday?" Gideon asked.

"All lined up. Everyone's excited about the surprise."

Gideon smiled, looking forward to seeing his plan implemented. "What's on your docket for today?"

"Depends on why you're askin'."

Gideon tried to laugh, but he didn't feel much like it. His attempt died before leaving his lips. "A long lunch and we need to sneak by Charisse's house, take an inventory on what we'll need for our little surprise."

"I had to close the door for that? Remind me you aren't much on tellin' a good yarn."

Gideon again closed his eyes, but at the soft rap on his door, he opened them. "Come on in."

"Good morning." Charisse stepped inside, a sight for sore, tired eyes—his dreams come to life. Except this morning, she was wearing a nice silver-gray blouse with a pair of navy slacks and jacket, looking more professional than many of the attorneys who stood before his bench. Too bad, her husband's death had prevented her from returning to law school. He needed to encourage her to continue with her studies.

"Morning." Gideon stood.

Charisse scanned him from head to foot as if seeking to find something wrong with him. Had he never stood when she entered?

A smile turned her lips and lit her beautiful blue eyes. "I didn't mean to interrupt you. I wanted to give you the research for this morning's hearing." She stepped forward with a file. "I'm sorry I didn't get it to you yesterday."

"Have I ever gotten upset about that before?" Gideon teased.

"Don't go there, Gid." She slapped the file against his chest.

"He's a bore." Deacon stepped away from the desk. A paper billowed to the ground, and Charisse bent to pick it up, her body turned away from them.

"Hey, old man." Gideon fell back into his chair.

Deacon waited.

Gideon looked at Charisse and back to his friend. "That question you asked me—I'm not sick."

Deacon laughed. "Masterful storytellin'. I'm looking forward to that long lunch when you can tell me the rest of it." He walked out, closing the door behind him.

"Aren't you feeling well?" Charisse put the paper back on his desk.

"I'm fine," he told her, cherishing her concern.

"Gideon, if you're sick, V.J. can go to a game with

you some other time."

Gideon stood again. He took her hand in his and placed it against his forehead. "See. No fever. I'm feeling wonderful, in fact. I can't wait to take Veej to the game."

"That's all he chattered about this morning." She pulled from his touch and ran her hand along the edge of his desk. She turned her gaze to the wall behind him. "Gideon, can I ask you to do something for me?"

"Anything." He waited, holding his breath. Had Delilah been right? Was Charisse going to break his heart before he even told her how he felt?

"Our working relationship is valuable to me, as valuable as our friendship once was."

Once was? Gideon released his breath. "Yes?"

"But if something should come up, and if we ever have a difference in opinion, please don't break my son's heart." She released a swoosh of breath. "He loves you. I don't know how you did it, but you've begun to piece together his little broken heart, and I can't bear to ever see it shattered again, at least by things within our control."

"Charisse, I—"

"Judge Tabor." The door into his courtroom opened and his bailiff entered. "Are you ready? The parties have arrived."

"Thank you. Apologize for the delay. I'll be right in."

Bill hesitated but closed the door.

"Charisse—" Gideon started.

"That's all. Whatever happens to our friendship, please don't hurt V.J." Her blue eyes pleaded with him.

"I'd never purposely hurt either of you." He gathered the research she'd prepared and then reached for her hand.

"We need to talk, don't we?"

Her nod surprised him. "Tonight, when I pick up V.J.?"

"Tonight." He released his touch. Tonight with God's help, he'd begin to heal her broken heart. If things turned out the way he planned, someday in eternity, he'd be able to thank Vance Wellman for allowing Gideon the privilege of caring for the wife and son he'd left behind. This workday couldn't get over fast enough for him.

FAY LAMB

Chapter Ten

The Amway Center was packed for the Orlando
Magic game. Gideon pointed toward his season seats.

V.J.'s awed eyes and smile grew even wider. He
tilted his head back to see the upper deck of the
auditorium and then looked down at the floor twelve rows
below. Gideon was sure he'd worn the same goofy
expression the first time he'd realized he'd purchased
such great seats. Finally, college and law school had paid
off big, if only in the wide-eyed gaze of a seven-year-old.

"Here." Gideon held V.J.'s hand and moved in front
of the boy. They squeezed past fans already seated in the
row. In the middle of the aisle, he sat and pushed down
another seat for V.J. The boy climbed around him and
plopped into it.

"Can you see?"

"Yes, sir." V.J. bounced in the chair, holding tightly
to the cap and shirt Gideon purchased for him. "Are these
really your seats?"

Gideon leaned toward him. "Yeah, but if word gets
out everyone will ask us for tickets, and these are ours,
right?"

"You mean you'll bring me again?"

"When it's not a school night, and if your mommy
says yes."

"If I do my homework, she'll let me."

Gideon couldn't help but grin. He rubbed the boy's head, and V.J.'s face beamed as he took in the rest of the stadium with that trusting look Cletus sometimes gave to Gideon.

The lights dimmed, the music blared, and the fans stood to cheer as spotlights ricocheted across the floor. Gideon picked up V.J. so he could see. When the lights brightened again, Gideon put the small boy down. V.J. scooted back into his seat. Gideon sat, nodding to the large, fearsome-looking fellow who owned the seats in front of him.

"So, when Mommy goes to her meetings, do you tag along?" Gideon asked.

"I don't go with her when she goes to talk about the union."

Union?

"It'd be boring listening to a bunch of old people talk about when they went to school," V.J. continued.

Reunion. Gideon smiled with sudden understanding.

Old people. Gideon guessed that in the eyes of a little boy he and Charisse were ancient.

"So mostly when Mommy goes to her union meeting, I go to my Mamaw's house," V.J. continued.

"Soda. Ice cold soda." A vendor walked the center aisle with a tray of drinks.

V.J. leaned around Gideon.

"Want one?" Gideon asked.

"No, sir."

"I'll get one, and we can share if you decide you want a drink." He held up his hand and motioned. The girl sent the plastic souvenir cup filled with soda down the row, and Gideon pulled out the money and passed it toward her. For once, he wished the cups came with a straw. Hmm. He guessed people with kids did see stuff like this in a different light. He shrugged and took the lid off and set it on the concrete floor, holding the moisture-covered cup. He'd just have to make sure that V.J. was careful with it.

"Where does Mommy go for her reunion meetings?"

V.J.'s attention turned from the game back to Gideon. "Huh?"

"Where does Mommy go for her reunion meetings?"

"Judge Tabor, I don't go. I said I stay with my Mamaw. I don't know where she goes."

Gideon fought to suppress his laughter. "Okay, fair enough."

Gideon sipped the soda and watched the game. On the large screen, they'd captured the perfect shot of some fan falling while trying to get to his seat. Gideon smiled. He'd never do something stupid enough that the camera would be turned on him.

"Why'd you want to know?" V.J. asked.

"Oh, I'm just trying to get to know you." *Yeah, I get it, Veej. We already know each other.*

V.J. stared at him. "People don't ask about us. Mommy says it's because they don't know how to ask about Daddy."

Gideon straightened. Even he hadn't pursued the subject past Charisse's declaration of an car accident. "I bet you miss him, huh?"

V.J. leaned closer to hear him above the roar of the crowd. He bit his lip and nodded his answer.

"Were you in the accident?"

V.J. continued to watch the game without providing an answer.

Please, dear Lord, tell me this boy didn't see his father die.

V.J. looked up at Gideon. "Daddy had picked up Mommy from school. They were on their way to pick me up. Mommy didn't come, but the ladies at daycare stayed with me. They told me Mommy would be there. Then Mamaw Taylor came to get me. She was crying, and it scared me. She told me Daddy had been *kilt*."

The crowd roared around them, and Gideon used the distraction to settle his own emotions. He could still remember the look on his mother's face when the doctor met them outside his father's hospital room and told them Dad had passed—he'd died in his sleep.

When the noise quieted, Gideon touched the boy's shoulder. "I bet it was scary. But you found out Mommy was okay?"

"She was sitting in the car." V.J. tilted his head. "Daddy was outside the car."

"Outside? Had the car broken down?"

"No. Somebody else's car was broke. Daddy liked to help people."

Gideon had a case like that once. A hit and run driver. The guy had stopped to aid an elderly man to change a tire. He'd finished and was about to get in his car when …

The case came rushing back to him. Young man. Left behind a wife and a son. The wife attended law school. Their son was five or six.

But the state attorney hadn't proven his case against the defendant. They couldn't place him at the scene. Gideon sensed the man they'd apprehended had something to do with the incident, but he doubted the man had been behind the wheel. He'd waited for the prosecutor to prove the state's case, and when he didn't, he was forced to …

Oh, Lord, no.

Gideon had entered a directed verdict against the man he believed was wrongly charged with running down— against the man charged with running over and leaving Vance Wellman, Sr., dead at the scene of the accident.

And he was sitting here beside Vance Wellman, Jr.

Gideon tightened his grip on the drink in his hand. The moisture buildup launched the cup upward. He tried to retrieve the wayward missile, bobbling it in the air. V.J. pulled back, protecting his new cap and shirt from the spillage.

Brown liquid cascaded over the burly man sitting in front of them. The cup landed top down with a plop on the guy's head.

"Oops," V.J. uttered as the man jumped to his feet, raising clenched fist and glaring at Gideon.

"What in the world! Hey, buddy, what are you doing?" The man shook like Cletus did after a bath. People around them murmured complaints.

Gideon stood in front of V.J., harboring him from any verbal or physical abuse.

Ice slid from the man's nose and ran into his beard. Soda dripped from his hair. Murmurs turned to laughter.

V.J. peered around Gideon. "He didn't mean to do it.

We're sorry."

The angry man turned his gaze upon the boy, and the face behind the scruffy beard softened. "I'm not going to beat up your daddy, son. Just relax. Accidents happen. The stuff was cold, that's all." He reached down in front of him and turned back with the cup in his hand. "You'll want to keep this to remember the game."

"Thank you." V.J. took the cup and scooted back into his chair.

Gideon dug in his wallet and pulled out a fifty-dollar bill. "Dinner after the game is on me. I am sorry."

"Put your money away." The man turned and sat down. Gideon fell into his seat, taking a few deep breaths to relieve the tension. He offered V.J. a smile he didn't feel.

Tears pooled in the boy's eyes.

Gideon gathered V.J. into his lap, and the boy leaned against him.

An overwhelming sense that Gideon needed—no, he wanted—to protect V.J. sent emotion welling to the surface. He blinked and then cleared his throat of emotion before saying, "It's okay. We worked it out. I made a mess. He had every right to get mad."

"He thinks you're my daddy." V.J. tucked his face against Gideon's shirt. The child's shoulders shook with his sobs.

Gideon's heart swelled, and the sounds of cheering fans seemed to fade into the distance. "I know you miss him, Veej." This little guy was grieving. Gideon needed to give him a chance to verbalize the sorrow, which came with both the good and the bad memories. "The key is to remember him." Gideon lifted V.J.'s chin with his finger. "Tell me something you remember about your daddy." *And while you do, I'll see if I can get rid of this sickening feeling that I've lost you and your mother before I get the chance to win her heart.*

Tears spilled down V.J.'s face. "We used to make up games." His lips trembled.

"What'd you play?"

"The kind of games you played with me in your office. One time he made us wooden swords, and we played pirates." V.J. beamed through his tears.

Gideon smiled. "Good memories, huh?"

V.J. nodded. "Judge Tabor?"

With a gentle thumb, Gideon wiped away the evidence of the boy's grief. "Yeah, Veej."

"Daddy wouldn't mind you being my daddy since he can't come home from heaven. I wish you were my 'nother daddy."

Gideon hugged V.J. to him and swallowed down the lump in his throat.

He adored this kid.

And he loved the boy's mother.

Charisse had to know he entered the directed verdict. He had so many cases before him, but he hadn't forgotten this one as easy as the others. The victim was mentioned, but he remembered cases by the defendant's name and by the facts presented in the case.

Carson Fullwell was the man charged. And the evidence presented against him was far from meeting the burden of proof placed upon the state attorney's office.

He leaned his head back and glanced up at the rafters.

After the way he'd treated Charisse in high school, why would she approach him? And after his most recent temper tantrum over the research, no wonder she was afraid to say anything.

The verdict. That was the reason for the distance she maintained. Better she erect a wall than allow her anger to spill over.

He had to admire her. *Charisse. Grace defined.*

"Judge Tabor?" V.J. looked up at him. "I'm sorry if you don't want to be my 'nother daddy. I won't ask again."

"Veej," Gideon ruffled the boy's hair. "Your father left behind a little guy I've grown to love very much. I'd be proud if God let me be your 'nother daddy."

V.J. nodded, and a single tear slid down his cheek. He leaned his head against Gideon's chest.

"I'm going to do my best to get Mommy to agree, but we need to pray and to remember that it's what God wants that's important. His plans for us are better than our own." *And I need Him to tear down a wall.*

Laughter erupted around them. People pointed to the monitor. On the screen, in replay, the burly man in front of them turned to look at Gideon, a scowl on his face, the soda all over his clothes, and droplets still in his hair. Gideon gulped air, afraid the attention might anger the guy again.

The man stood and then turned to face them, a scowl on his face. Then the big fellow's lips turned upward into a genuine smile. He raised a high five. Gideon stood with V.J. in his arms and slapped the guy's hand.

The crowd around them roared, and in Gideon's hold,

a little boy laughed with grand abandon.

Charisse carried her files and a calendar into the Titusville library and dumped them on the nearest table. She sat and began to organize her notes.

"Charisse, you're here." Libby tripped over a chair leg, and Charisse reached out to keep her from falling. Libby's RSVP slips drifted through the air, swaying to the floor around them.

Charisse knelt beside her friend.

Libby's brown hair fell over her large rimmed glasses as she scrambled to help pick up her mess. "Have you straightened out the biblical scenario, or is Gideon still in the dark?"

"Status quo."

Libby got to her feet and then plopped into a nearby chair. "You do realize in this situation you're the Delilah?"

Charisse stood and took a seat beside her. "That's not true." She worked with Libby to slip the papers back into alphabetical order.

Libby leaned back and stared at her. "Well, it's not like you're trying to take his strength from him or anything like that, but you're keeping something from him, knowledge that might make him a stronger judge."

"Stop with the guilt trip. I don't know how to tell Gid, and Delilah James is a problem. If she finds out I took the job knowing Gideon entered that verdict, she'd make it seem as if I'm waiting for a chance to stick a knife in his back."

Libby gasped. "You aren't that angry with him?"

Charisse sighed. "Not any longer. I allowed my pain to cloud my memories of the man Gideon has always been."

"Let God lead." Libby touched Charisse's hand. "I can't believe the woman I spoke to on the phone would harm you. She was nice."

"You always find something kind to say about everyone."

"Well, she seemed to show a genuine interest in everything about you."

"To use as ammunition." Charisse straightened. "Libby, what kind of questions did she ask?"

"She asked what year we graduated, what you were like in school."

"Did you mention I was overweight?"

"No. That never crossed my mind. You are always so beautiful—no matter what you weigh."

Charisse swallowed. Vance was the only other person who said that about her.

No, that wasn't true. Gideon said it the other night. Obviously, she wasn't beautiful enough. He couldn't wait for the reunion where he would see the woman he had loved.

"She seemed to genuinely like you, and when she asked for the website for our class reunion, I gave it to her."

Charisse tensed. "The website. My school photo is right beneath Gid's. Libby, he didn't tell Delilah anything about me. She saw my picture. That devious witch looked on the web page, and she's craftier than I thought."

"Now, Charisse, you just called her a witch."

Charisse leaned toward her friend. "No, I didn't." She laughed. "I called her a devious witch."

"You should be ashamed. We are to return good for evil." Libby's attempt at making an angry face failed, and they fell into a fit of laughter.

"Oh, my." Karen entered the room followed by Debbie and Pearl. "Charisse arrived before us. We should celebrate with ice cream at the Moonlight if we can get this meeting wrapped up early."

"Wrapped up?" Charisse helped Libby gather her stuff. Then she picked up her purse and folder. "We can meet there. Last one to arrive pays." And tonight she had the money to back up her wager. Still, she was the first one to her car, and the first one out of the parking lot.

The Moonlight Drive-In had long been a favorite spot for Titusville teens and adults, eating in the small dining area or enjoying a meal curbside. Charisse hadn't eaten there in some time.

Once the group gathered in the small dining room, Charisse took a moment to check out the décor. The black and white checkered floor remained, but since her last visit, the owners had hung an Elvis clock, his hips swiveling away the seconds. An Elvis cardboard cutout stood beside the emergency exit. Memorabilia from the 1950s and '60s adorned the walls: old 45s, a gold record from Elvis, pictures of James Dean, John Wayne, The Beatles, and Marilyn Monroe. Vintage album covers from groups like the Supremes, The Animals, and Herman's Hermits were stapled to the ceiling tiles.

Charisse ordered her favorite, a chilidog with cheese and onions and the best sweet tea in the South and waited for the others to make their requests.

They chatted until they finished eating. Then Karen got down to business. "Okay, we're getting closer here. Three weeks. What do we have?"

Debbie nearly bounced in her seat. "The napkins are printed. The cups are ready, and I have the door prizes all lined up. The grand prize will be the cruise I mentioned—for two—six days, seven nights in the Caribbean."

"Let's hope a married couple wins," Libby said.

"Why?" Debbie asked. "A single person could take a friend."

"Yeah," Charisse nudged Libby. "I'll take you. V.J. would love to stay with Gid—I mean, my boss."

"If he *stays* your boss." Libby gave her a wide-eyed glare.

"Whoa. Trouble on the job?" Pearl asked."

"Whoa, nothing." Debbie pointed. "Gid, as in Gideon Tabor? You little holdout. You're working for him, aren't you?"

Charisse wasn't sure, but if her face was as red as the burning in her cheeks indicated, she probably looked like one of those Atomic Red Fireballs she used to love to suck on while she watched her favorite quarterback on the football field.

"You are. I can tell. You're working for him. How could you keep that from us?" Debbie leaned back in her chair, arms folded.

"He's my boss. End of story." Charisse sipped her tea. Out of the corner of her eye, she caught a pointed glare from Libby. "Okay, as far as my agenda goes, Libby needs to contact Royal Oak Country Club to verify the entrees and the attendance a week before. They'll adjust for last minute attendees. We can go in early Saturday afternoon to decorate. The best plan would be to meet somewhere to put the decorations together so it will be easier for us to load and take to the country club."

"We can use my house." Libby offered. "Even if I'm in Orlando with my mother, I can give the key to Charisse."

Charisse touched Libby's hand. "You've worked hard, and you're going to take part in this reunion whether or not your mother is in the hospital."

"I don't see how."

"Let God lead. Isn't that what you told me earlier?"

Libby nodded. "The good news is we received ten more RSVPs. I think this reunion is going to be one of the best ever."

Charisse continued to drink her sweet tea and looked to each of her friends. With the knowledge they'd just obtained, she and Gideon weren't safe from their meddling. They could destroy Gideon's chances with his ladylove. The thought was enough to make her want to order a banana split with nothing but hot fudge and whipped cream for the toppings. Whether it was to celebrate the meddling or to commiserate her loss, she wasn't sure.

She looked around the table. The other three women were eyeing each other. Libby was staring at her. They wouldn't let this matter rest. The time had come. She needed to talk to Gideon. She would have to face her emotions: anger, hurt, remorse.

And an incredible amount of love.

Chapter Eleven

Gideon hung up his phone and smiled at V.J. "Your mom said she'd be about thirty minutes." He moved into his kitchen. V.J. hadn't heard a word he said. Boy and dog romped in Gideon's living room, and he didn't know who enjoyed the friendship the most, the kid or the hound.

He reached into his freezer and surveyed the ice cream boxes. "Veej, vanilla okay?"

"That's fine, Judge Tabor."

"Want some chocolate syrup?"

"Uh-huh." V.J. clomped into the kitchen with Cletus on his heels.

"Go wash your hands. No telling what he's been into." Gideon pointed toward the bathroom, and V.J. started away. "Hey."

V.J. turned.

"I was talking to Cletus."

The boy giggled as he and the dog ran in the same direction. Gideon pulled two bowls from the cabinet and picked up Cletus's dog dish. When V.J. returned, they sat at the kitchen table and left Cletus in the corner lapping his dish of ice cream, minus the topping.

"Thank you, Judge Tabor. I had a really good time."

Poised and direct. His mother had taught him well.

"What did you like best?" Gideon asked.

"The slam dunks they made."

"I noticed you didn't care which team made them. You cheered every time." Even the bearded man in his soda-soaked clothing had turned to smile at the boy.

V.J. nodded as he ate. He wiped a stray drop of ice cream from his chin. "Judge Tabor?"

"You can call me Gid or Gideon."

"Mommy said no."

Gideon stopped the growl from escaping. He did need to break down the wall Charisse wanted to keep between them. "Okay, until Mommy and I talk. Now, what were you asking?"

"Did you really mean it when you said you want to be my 'nother daddy?"

What had he said in the heat of the moment with V.J.'s sad eyes staring up at him?

The subject needed to change.

"V.J., your mother told me something that has me perplexed. Maybe you can help me out with it."

Cletus finished his ice cream and came to sit beside V.J.'s chair, resting his nose on the boy's lap.

"I'll try if you tell me what *preplexed* means." V.J. stroked the dog's head.

"Perplexed means confused. Mommy says you're a sad guy. I see it sometimes, like tonight. But I don't see it as much as she does. I like to hang out with you because you laugh at my jokes, and you make me laugh. Is there a robot Veej you hide in a corner for Mommy to see, and I get the real Veej or ..." Gideon hoped to see a smile on the boy's face. He was disappointed. V.J.'s stare screamed silent pain, and for the first time, Gideon saw what Charisse faced daily. "Okay, not too funny. Sorry."

"Is Mommy mad at me?"

Gideon shook his head to answer the boy's question and get his brain to follow V.J.'s train of thought. "Not at all. She's worried. What makes you think she's mad?"

"Judge Tabor, if I tell you, you won't tell her, will you?"

"No. Go ahead."

"Mommy's mad at my daddy, and I don't know how to stop her from being mad."

"What do you mean?"

"She yells at him."

Gideon had gotten himself in over his head. What in the world made him think he could counsel the little guy? V.J. was smarter than him. He waited for the boy to continue.

"I heard her scream all the way to heaven because Daddy helped that man on the road. Daddy didn't know he'd be *kilt*. He wouldn't of done it if he knew. Mommy cried and said she hated him. I never saw her cry so hard before. I called my Mamaw, and she told me I shouldn't listen to Mommy because she's very sad."

Gideon cleared emotion from his throat. V.J. had just described the Charisse he knew and loved—the little girl who released her pain in the same way. "You do realize your mom loves your dad very much?"

"She's so mean to him now, though. She blames him because he stopped and helped the man."

How did you tell a little boy anger was a stage of grief, and Charisse didn't mean a word she said? "So, you don't buy Mamaw's explanation?"

"I don't think so. If you were sad, would you get

mad?"

Gideon smiled. Way back when, God had been preparing him—and Charisse—for this precise moment. "V.J., when my dad died, I was a little older than you but still a kid. He'd been sick for a long time, but he didn't tell anyone. When he died, it was as sudden to me as your dad's death. I was very angry with him."

"What'd you do?" V.J. straightened in his chair.

"A good friend took me for a ride in her car. We went out by the Indian River."

"Mamaw lives on the Indian River."

Gideon nodded. "Well, one night this girl drove me over the bridge past the fishing pier. Do you know where that is?"

V.J. nodded.

"And this friend listened to me tell her about my father and how angry I was at him. Then she told me her father just walked away and never came home. She said her dad hurt her very badly when he left. Then she showed me how she dealt with her sadness."

"How?"

"She screamed into the darkness. She told her father what she thought of him for leaving her and her mother. She said she hated him."

Gideon's smile vanished at the memory. All screamed out, Charisse had cried against him. She'd felt so right in his arms. Her young girl heart only wanted answers, and he'd been unable to give her a reason why a father would leave such a wonderful daughter.

"Did you scream at your daddy, too?"

"Oh, like your dad, my father got to hear all about my

anger. I asked him how he could leave me. I told him I hated him for lying to me about being sick. I let him know how I felt about the things he'd miss in my life."

V.J.'s eyes grew round.

"Then, I cried, and I told him how much I loved him."

"Did the girl tell her daddy how much she loved him?"

Gideon wouldn't lie to the kid. "No." He leaned toward V.J. and gave him a little nudge with his elbow. "But I bet she tells your daddy every night."

V.J. looked puzzled for a moment—but only a moment. The kid was bright. "The girl was Mommy?"

"And she's worried about you, Veej. You gotta take my word for it. Your dad and her father were different people. She knows your dad was being the kind, generous man I suspect he was. She's not really angry with him. She's upset he had to leave you, and if your dad can hear her, he knows the only reason she's yelling at him is because she loves and misses him. She's not angry with you either, but she misses the little boy you used to be. She sees your droopy face and doesn't know how to bring her old Veej back to her. She wants to see you smile."

"I want Mommy to smile, too. She laughs with you, Judge Tabor. I like it when she laughs."

Gideon tapped his fingers on the table. There had to be a way to make Charisse happy.

I knew I loved him because he made me forget this idiot I loved who never showed any real interest in me in high school.

I guess if the idiot came up to you and asked you to

marry him, you'd say no?

I don't know. I gave the guy four years of my life, and he never noticed.

What a fool.

You said it, not me.

Gideon stopped his tapping. His eyes widened. Charisse had given him four years of her life. Hadn't she ever noticed the way he searched her out, followed her around, pretended he couldn't catch on to a subject when he probably could have tutored others instead of playing the dunce? He'd done it all to have her near him.

Yet she'd been so hurt by his carelessness that she'd called him an idiot—and she'd loved him. She never knew his feelings for her, that they ran deep and swift.

He'd practically told her the truth. And she didn't catch on.

His laughter spilled out.

V.J. leaned away from him. "Judge Tabor, are you okay?"

"Yeah, sorry. I just thought of something funny."

"What?" His little boy eyes stared up at him.

"Like your little setup for your teacher, your mommy isn't going to see me coming. We still have to pray about it, but do you want to hear my plan?"

Charisse stopped in front of Gideon's condo door. She brushed her sweaty palms against her skirt then knocked.

Gideon opened the door and put a finger to his lips.

She stepped inside and smiled. V.J. and Cletus slept side by side on an air mattress in Gideon's living room. V.J.'s lips turned upward in a contented smile.

"Would you like something to drink?" Gideon asked.

She shook her head. "I had a humongous tea at the Moonlight."

"Yeah? Really? Love that place."

"May I use your restroom?"

He offered her a knowing smile. "Long drive?"

"Yes." She squirmed.

He pointed down a long hallway. "How about some ice cream?"

She widened her eyes. "I splurged on a banana split along with a chilidog with cheese and onions." She placed her hands over her stomach. "I'm afraid I ate too much." She moved into his bathroom and closed the door. Why did she insist on drinking the entire jumbo sweet tea and ordering a second to drink on the way home—on top of the ice cream? Her stomach ached. She was no longer a teenager, but having the money to splurge had felt so good she'd overindulged.

When she stepped out, Gideon was sitting at his kitchen counter.

He pulled out a chair beside him and she sat. "The Moonlight does serve the best chili-cheese dogs and sweet tea. I always top off the meal with a hot fudge sundae or a milkshake."

Charisse put her fingers to her lips, squelching the unlady-like belch forming deep within. She swallowed and offered him a nod.

A smile flitted at the corner of his lips and then

faded. "How are you feeling?"

"Honestly, I'm tired." Though not a lie, it was an evasive tactic. She'd spent the entire drive here debating on whether to discuss the trial and his verdict. She couldn't do it. Not here. Not after he'd been so kind to her son.

She looked at her little boy who slept on the air mattress. She hadn't seen him smile in his sleep since before Vance's death.

"Then let me do the talking, will you? I won't take too long." Gideon regained her attention.

She nodded.

"I told you about the crush I had on my high school friend."

She shifted in her seat, looking everywhere but at Gideon.

"And the reunion's coming up."

She waited, breath tight in her throat. How had he learned about this woman's attendance? Libby said they had ten new RSVPs. Was Gideon's fantasy one of those? But who would he have asked for the information?

"Charisse, I know you can't help but notice. My feelings for you and for V.J. are strong ones, and they're growing every day."

"Yes," she managed to say.

"And if I thought there's a chance you could feel the same way I'm beginning to feel about you …"

"Gideon, you need to forget about me. Get to know this woman. I come with too much baggage and a son."

"I plan on meeting with this girl. I have to. I've loved the idea of what she was for so long."

Charisse fought to hide her tears. Gideon's heart could soon be lost to her forever if she couldn't forgive and forget.

"I don't want to give half of my heart to Charisse Wellman." He touched her hand. "I want to give it all to you and to your son. But I need to face my past. Then everything will become clear. I know I shouldn't ask, but can you give me until our reunion, let me confront some issues so I can truly tell you my heart belongs to you?"

"Gid," she breathed his name. "I need to tell you something."

He pressed his finger against her lips. "You don't have to say anything to me."

"But really. You should know something."

"Charisse." His green eyes searched hers. "Don't worry about it." He leaned forward.

Charisse hiccupped and covered her mouth.

A smile touched his lips as he leaned even closer. Would he kiss her? Oh, why had she eaten a chili dog with cheese … and onions.

Gideon touched his forehead to hers and turned to look at V.J. "I love V.J. I'm never going to hurt him. If things don't work out between us, I'll always be there for him."

Charisse kept her hand over her lips to keep him from being knocked back by her breath. "Your friend might not understand."

"As sure as I am that she'll be attending our reunion, I'm one-hundred percent sure she'll always love V.J. as much as I do."

Charisse turned her head, still pressed close to

Gideon. Her gaze rested upon her sleeping son. She didn't want another woman to love him. She wanted to love him with Gideon, train him in the integrity Vance instilled in him and Gideon could reinforce.

She closed her eyes and took a deep breath.

"I can see you're exhausted. Why don't you let Veej stay over? We're supposed to meet in the park tomorrow anyway. I have some plans early in the morning with some of the people from the office. Can he tag along with me?"

Her heart was either a traitorous blood-pumping organ or, despite everything, she trusted Gideon Tabor with her most important possession. "I'll meet you at the park."

He offered her a warm smile. "Don't worry about this too much. After all, the girl I once knew could have changed. I mean really changed."

Charisse picked up her purse and trudged toward the door. She stopped and looked back at her little boy nestled on the bed beside Gideon's overgrown mutt.

"She might not be as pretty as I remember her or as sweet and caring. She might be a totally different person," Gideon continued.

One could only hope.

Or more aptly, as Libby would no doubt remind her: she could pray.

A momentary surge in faith tipped the corners of Charisse's lips upward.

Chapter Twelve

The whirl of the engine and the hum of other machinery drifted into Charisse's dreams. She opened one eye and stared at the alarm clock. Three hours of sleep before some maniac neighbor decided to disturb the entire block with his yard work.

She rolled over, slapping her arms down against the mattress. "It's Saturday. A person should be able to sleep."

"Morning, Mommy."

Charisse jumped at V.J's cheery voice. Had she dreamed last night? Had there been no class reunion meeting to fuel thoughts of Gideon telling her he had to make sure he didn't love another first? No V.J. staying with Gid?

V.J. carried a tray of food to her.

She pushed herself up. "What's this?"

"Judge Tabor fixed it for you. He said you're to eat every bit of it before you come downstairs, and you aren't supposed to help."

"Help what?" Charisse brought the covers up over her. Gideon was here, in her house? She ran a hand through her tangle of curls.

"Bill!" The shout came from outside. "Move that old wood trim from that weed garden."

"Is that Judge Foster?"

V.J. nodded.

"What's going on here?"

"I'm not allowed to tell, and you can't get up and see until you've eaten everything. Judge Tabor said so."

"V.J., how'd you get in?"

"I showed Judge Tabor where we keep our outside key."

Of course he had.

Charisse looked at her plate. Her eyes feasted upon scrambled eggs, bacon, grits, a tomato, buttered toast—not even slightly burnt—and a cup of coffee. "Have you eaten?" she asked.

He nodded. "Hurry and come see who all is here. There're lots of people."

"Lots of people?" She started to push the tray away.

"Uh-uh, Charisse." Gideon leaned in the doorway, filling the entrance with his presence. "I was afraid you wouldn't listen to my *temporary* second in command. "Eat. Then come down."

He was tall and handsome, and his smile stole her heart. But he wasn't hers—and with the odds and the facts against her, she'd probably never be his.

"Come on, Veej. We have a lot of work to do if we're going to make it to the park." He gave her a crooked grin. "Cletus is here. I hope you don't mind."

"You looked after my kid. I'm happy to look after yours." She chomped on her toast.

"Ask a blessing over your food first." He pointed at her. "And don't come down those stairs until your plate is clean."

"Yes, sir."

She started to hurry through the meal, but the food tasted so good, she had to savor it. When was the last time anyone had cooked for her?

Outside, machinery hummed and voices called to one another.

"You all get them there weeds around the mailbox." Marlene's Georgia accent filled the air. "And V.J., you put on some gloves."

Charisse relaxed. Her son was in good hands.

She relished the meal, and when she finished, she dressed and went downstairs.

Cletus met her in the foyer, his ears perked up then lowered. Curiosity tilted his head with each new sound, and there were lots of them: chain saws, clippers, hedge trimmers, and a lawn mower. She bent down and petted him, receiving a warm lick on her cheek. She buried her head against his fur. "I love you, too, boy."

"Woof," Cletus answered.

With one more pat of his head, she opened her front door and moved onto her porch. Cletus stood guard beside her.

An army of people bustled about, weeding the flower gardens, trimming her trees, cleaning her gutters, and a myriad of other details she never accomplished.

"Hey." Marlene dropped her hoe into the dirt and walked up to her. "We don't want you lifting a hand out here. Gideon told us how sick you got the last time." She motioned to Gideon who pruned a bougainvillea bush at the side of her house.

Working with the thorny plant, Gideon was sure to need a first-aid kit by the end of the day.

"This is a wonderful surprise, but why are you all here?" Charisse asked.

"Hello, darling." Judge Foster's clerk, Zelma, waved and then lifted the Marlin's baseball cap from atop her gray hair. She swiped the sweat from her forehead and replaced the hat.

"Why not, Charisse? We love you." Marlene leaned against the porch railing.

A woman pushed a wheelbarrow full of yard debris across the driveway.

"Crystal?" Charisse gaped at Delilah's clerk.

"Yeah, well, I had to shame her into coming, but she's enjoying herself." Marlene scrunched up her nose.

"I should help."

"No." Gideon's voice boomed. "If you want to be helpful, pack us a cooler filled with lunches. After we're done here, we're all going to go home, change, and meet up at Lake Eola."

"It's a fun day, Mommy." V.J. waved from the now empty wheelbarrow Crystal pushed back across the yard. A huge smile filled his cute little face.

Emotion welled inside of Charisse. She let out a small cry and put her hand over her mouth. She stumbled backward, tears blurring her vision.

"Hey." Gideon dropped his pruning saw and ran to her. "You okay?"

She shook her head, and the tears spilled down her cheeks.

Cletus lifted a paw to her waist, and caught off guard, Charisse fell against the wall.

Gideon slipped an arm around her waist and led her

inside. "Cletus," he commanded the dog to follow before shutting the door. He moved with her to the couch. "What is it?"

"I'm—I'm so overwhelmed." She sank to the cushion. "All these wonderful people—V.J.—and you won't let me help?"

"You can hardly stand."

"Because I'm surprised." She half-cried, half-laughed, swatting at him.

"You can help. Give it a little while and then fix us lunches for the picnic at the park."

Her eyes pooled with tears. "I can't."

He bent in front of her. "Are you that weak? I'm worried about you."

She stared into his green eyes. He didn't need to tell her he was anxious about her health. She saw it in their wonderful expressiveness, and his concern wrenched her heart. "It's not that at all. As nice as all of you are being to me, I don't have the food to fix that many lunches."

He held both her hands in his. "Here's what I want you to do."

Charisse lifted her gaze to the ceiling to keep the tears from falling again.

"Are you listening?"

She nodded and turned her attention back to him.

"I want you to sit here and pray real hard for God's solution to your dilemma. Pray until you are confident God has provided. Then I want you to walk in that kitchen and get to work."

She didn't answer.

"Pray and believe." He left her.

Charisse sat for a few minutes. What good would a prayer do? She'd invited both Gideon and Judge Foster for lunch the next day, and she had planned her groceries around the meal, hoping to stretch the ingredients to cook several casseroles for her and V.J. to eat throughout the week. She couldn't go to the store and spend money on lunches for today.

Maybe if she hadn't splurged on the food she'd eaten during last night's meeting. How long had it been since she'd done something for herself? Now the guilt plagued her. She could have used the money she wasted to provide for those helping her today.

What little hope she had that things were beginning to turn around faded. When had she lost so much of her faith in God and his provision for her?

She leaned forward and cried into her hands. "Dear God, help me overcome my unbelief. Why, even in the midst of Your goodness, do I fret over what's already been done? Gideon could have given me the money to buy the food, but his faith is so strong, he wants me to pray. Lord, show me how to believe in Your promises. Walk me out of this bottomless pit of doubt and fill me with the conviction that You provide all things. In Your way and in Your time, You will supply all my needs."

She sat in silence for a long while. Still, the doubt remained.

Well, she had to scrape together something. Maybe if she went light on the peanut butter and jelly and cut the sandwiches in half she could make enough. She'd give them each two or three potato chips, but what would she do for drinks?

She pushed herself from the couch and walked into the kitchen. She gazed through her window at Deacon Foster planting flowers in what was once Vance's showcase garden. Now it was being transformed back into the beauty Vance had designed.

Crystal came from the side. V.J. tagged along with her. They picked up the debris and placed it in the wheelbarrow.

How could she allow them to do so much and provide them so little in return?

She moved to the refrigerator, dreading the emptiness she knew lay inside. "Dear God, make it full. Make it full. Please make it full," she whispered and pulled the door open.

Her mouth hung open. She reached inside. Milk, butter, eggs, juice, a variety of vegetables, and sandwich meats filled the refrigerator to overflowing. She pulled open the freezer. Frozen vegetables, meats, and ice cream—her favorite, vanilla with cookie dough—packed the shelves. She closed the doors and moved to the pantry. "Coffee—wondrous coffee—a variety of canned sodas, canned vegetables, pastas, salad oils, condiments, and cheese puffs—she loved cheese puffs. She ate bags of them in high school. Gideon had remembered. "Oh." She reached and touched the large containers of peanut butter and jelly. "Full. All full."

"Look at that," Gideon said from the kitchen door. "God does answer prayers."

She ran to him.

"Oomph." He caught her as she threw her arms around him, not caring that he was sweaty and grimy.

"Thank you, Gideon. Thank you."

He brushed a kiss across the top of her hair. "I'll take that reward any time, but it doesn't belong to me, Charisse. God has supplied your need. I just happened to need a few things when I fixed your breakfast."

"A few things? Gideon this is a treasure house of food."

"All sent to you by God's hand, Charisse Wellman."

But God used Gideon Tabor to provide for her, and she clung to him.

How would she ever let him go?

Chapter Thirteen

Charisse pushed open the door to her back porch and drank in the smell of fresh cut grass and newly turned soil. She sneezed.

At least if she gained a migraine, it wouldn't be because she'd done the heavy labor. As she walked into the yard, memories of Vance weaved through her mind like the trimmed honeysuckle clinging to the trellis.

Vance had purchased the house for the potential beauty he saw in the yard. He designed the pathways and the gardens, leaving space for V.J. to play. He'd spent hours tending to the yard with such care. He even planted the azaleas she asked for, but over the last year, those had withered and died without him.

And the man upstairs, the one who asked if he could shower and change in her home had orchestrated this return of the beauty she'd allowed to fade.

Charisse chuckled as Cletus pounced on a beetle in the grass. "Get it boy." Her eyes swept across her yard once again. "It's so beautiful," she whispered.

"We wanted it to be beautiful for you. Deacon and I sneaked over here yesterday at lunch and took inventory." Gideon stood behind her.

She could feel his warmth. He placed his hands on her shoulders. Her vanilla-scented soap he used tickled her senses.

"Marlene said this would be a beautiful place for a wedding."

His statement struck her like lightning and mixed with the thundering of her heart. "Who's getting married?" She leaned back and looked up into his handsome face.

He smiled down at her. "Oh, I don't know. Marlene seemed to have a vivid plan for the event. Chairs on each side of the path, the bride walking down the aisle, the groom standing there," he nodded to the right side of the honeysuckle-filled trellis, "by the pastor."

"What colors?" She looked where his gaze remained. "Hmm?"

"Vivid plans include the bride's colors."

He shrugged. "I don't know. What colors would you like for a wedding?"

"Yellow and black." She answered too quickly—the slight tightening of his grasp on her shoulders told her so.

"I graduated from the University of Florida, Charisse. I'm a Gator fan. Those are Georgia Tech colors."

"Well you can have an orange and blue wedding if you want, but not me."

"Tell me more." He took her hand and moved to a double swing she'd watched Gideon and Deacon hang from the heavy limb of the old oak. "You like?" he asked.

"I love it." She sat and he followed, sitting beside her in the snug two-seater.

"Yellow and black, I'm listening."

She closed her eyes and leaned against the seat.

Gideon put the swing in motion.

"Yellow roses." Like the ones he'd gifted her. "My

bridesmaids will wear beautiful yellow dresses. I'll wear a soft cream dress, and my groom and his groomsmen will wear black tuxes with light yellow cummerbunds."

"Wow, is that from your wedding to Vance?"

She opened her eyes. "No. It's only a dream." Yet, in her imaginings, Gideon had been her groom. She lowered her eyes and took a deep breath. "Just a dream, Gid. That's all."

"And why a cream dress and not a white one?"

The warmth of a blush caressed her cheeks "Gideon, why are we talking about this? If Marlene would like to use my yard for a wedding, she's more than welcome."

Gideon slowed the swing and brought it to a halt. "Marlene is married. You met her husband. I think she's planning one for someone very special."

"Then I'll let her know my yard is available." She stood and spun away from him.

"Charisse?" He caught her by the arm.

She looked up into his serious eyes. "Yes," she whispered, hoping he'd forgotten about the mysterious woman who planned to attend the reunion. *Dear Lord, help me to forgive this man completely. I know how much I stand to lose if my heart continues to scamper back to the bitterness its held for so long.*

Gideon's lips turned upward into one of his gorgeous smiles, and his dimples deepened. "Wear white in your dream wedding."

Beyond the picnic table, Lake Eola glistened in the

early afternoon sun. Gideon tossed the Frisbee to V.J. and turned to watch the boy's mother say good-bye to the departing crowd. Marlene and her husband, Crystal, several court clerks, and Bill the bailiff and his wife, left together.

Finally, Deacon kissed Charisse on the cheek. "See you tomorrow for dinner, darlin'."

Charisse held to the old man for a long moment. The sight warmed Gideon. Today, he and many friends helped mend a few pieces of her heart, and her reaction to the food in her cupboards was more than he could handle. How long had she struggled to keep groceries in the house for her and V.J.? Well, if he could help it, those days were over.

"Judge Tabor, are you going to throw me the Frisbee?" V.J. called.

Gideon turned and looked around him. The toy lay at his feet. He scooped it up. "Here, Veej. Let me go help Mommy." He gave the Frisbee a gentle toss. "Hey," he said to her, and picked up some of the condiments to put into the cooler. "Great lunch."

"Gideon, this was a wonderful day. I've never felt so special."

"I'm sure that's not true." He reached for her hand and turned the wedding band around. "Vance must have made every day special for you."

She stared down at his finger touching the ring then pulled her hand back.

"I know the truth." He reached for her again.

She jerked her gaze to his. "About what?"

"Why have you kept quiet? Is it because you're angry with me about my directed verdict?"

She winced and tears shined in her eyes—and this time they weren't from happiness or surprise. She lowered her head and droplets watered the ground. "Why?"

"Why am I asking now, or why did I do what I did?" He held to her hand like a lifeline. If he released her, he'd lose her. That's how he saw it.

With her free hand, she wiped at the tears. "I haven't had a lot of faith lately, Gid, but since I've taken this job, I've despised you at times, and I've forgiven you at others. I keep handing it over to God."

"Despised?"

She didn't speak.

"Let's talk now. We need to clear the air."

"Have you known this entire time?" She raised her teary blue eyes to him.

He reached for a paper towel and dabbed at her face. "No. Veej mentioned how so few people talk to him about his dad. I decided time had come to give the kid a chance to share some memories. When he told me about the accident, I recognized the facts of the case."

"That's just it. To you they're simply facts relayed to you by counsel and witnesses. To V.J. and me they're a reality we face every day, and I can't understand how you could devalue Vance's life so much that you'd let his killer go free."

"Let me ask you a question, and if you need time to think about it, tell me. You don't have to come up with the answer today. And you don't have to come up with the answer you think I'd like to hear or an answer you think Vance would want you to give. I want Charisse's answer."

She bit into her lower lip and nodded.

"Would you want an innocent person to pay for the crimes of another even if you suspected the man charged with your husband's death knew more than he was telling?"

She looked to the heavens and then beyond him to the lake.

He turned and followed her gaze out to the swan paddleboats and the people enjoying the day.

"I know I've hurt you before, Charisse. And I'm bound to hurt you again. I'm a man. I've been told we aren't very bright, but I'm going to be honest with you right now. If I had to make the same decision, I'd make the same call, for two reasons."

"Because they couldn't place him at the scene?" She gave her full attention to him. "But it was his car. He hadn't reported it stolen. He didn't say he'd loaned it to anyone."

"He also wasn't required to testify, and when the state ended its case, they hadn't met the burden of proof."

She tensed. Her hold on his hand tightened. "But so few motions for a directed verdict are entered."

"That's true, and with that in mind, do you think I'd ever take the verdict out of the jury's hands if I thought my action would be appealed? I'm a young man to have been appointed circuit court judge. I didn't take the honor lightly, and I decided when I campaigned to keep my job and won the election that I would uphold my office."

She nodded. "What was your second reason?"

"Because by entering a directed verdict of not guilty and dismissing the case against a person I felt wrongly accused, I left the door open for the state to discover the truth and investigate the case thoroughly and perhaps charge the right individual."

"But they haven't been looking into it."

"If I could ethically go to the state attorney and push for an investigation, I would. For you. Only for you and for Veej."

She relaxed, her hold on his hand lessening, her shoulders falling. A sad smile lifted the lines around her lips. "You and Vance would have been good friends, Gideon Tabor."

"I'm sure we would." He held up her hand and again fingered the ring before releasing his hold. "Are you ever going to take it off?"

"I never think of the ring. Like Vance, it's a part of me." She looked beyond him a second time, out to the swan boats. He again followed her gaze and let it linger there. When he turned back to her, she held her wedding band in her open hand. She closed her fingers around it. "You have to know. I loved Vance with every ounce of my being. He loved me for who I was and what I'd become. He loved me so well."

Gideon looked to the heavens, silently cursing the emotions fanning across his longing heart. If God allowed, he'd love her more.

"I'm praying for God to direct your path, and if the girl you loved is the one you're supposed to be with, I'm asking God to clear your way."

He swallowed the lump in his throat. Charisse wasn't getting it. How could she not understand that the woman she was and the woman she'd become had merged into the one woman he loved now?

Last night, he suspected his hints had been ineffective. The wall between them had begun to fall in, but enough of her defenses still remained to keep her heart from seeing the truth. "Are you telling me I have no chance with you?"

She opened her hand and stared once again at the ring. "I do need to have some closure, and I won't lie to you. When I think of Carson Fullwell walking past me after your dismissal of his case, it infuriates me." She gripped the ring and then gave a half-laugh. "Vance would want me to forgive. Whenever I stubbornly held to a grudge, he'd tell me I needed to live up to my name."

"You are the most gracious woman I know."

"On the outside, Gideon, but not on the inside. My stubborn refusal to offer grace to my husband weighs heavily on me. He died before I could apologize for being angry with him. Maybe my hardness toward you and Mr. Fullwell is a reflection on my own failures."

"I wish I could help you."

She touched his face. "This woman you're looking to connect with at the reunion doesn't know how blessed she can be. How could she have not known you loved her? You wear your heart on your sleeve."

He smiled and leaned his forehead against hers. "I don't know. It's a mystery to me." He covered the ring in her hand with his touch. "I meant what I said last night. Let me follow through. Something tells me that once I have the past behind me, I'll be looking to the future with you."

A tentative smile touched her lips. "Something deep inside hopes that's the truth, but I have to know that my emotions won't ricochet from one extreme to the other and hurt you. And I can't discard the fact that you might love someone else. You have to see this other woman. Otherwise, you may miss out on God's choice for you. And well, if I lose you, while I'm trying to get my love for you in focus, we'll know God had other plans for each of us."

He stepped away from her, the concern she held for him making him feel like a heel. At the same time his heart screamed the truth Charisse couldn't hear through her pain. *She loves me.* The thought came like a tiny whisper then a thundered voice that reverberated happiness through is entire being. *Oh, yes, she loves me!*

He rushed back to her, encircling her with his arms.

She leaned her head against his chest. Then she pulled away, her lips forming a perfect O. "I—I shouldn't have done that. I'm sorry."

"Charisse, if you tell me right now you don't want me to look her up, I won't give it another thought." He brushed her hair with his hand. "You can have my whole heart right this minute. It's yours for the taking. I can take your ricocheting emotions. I'm strong enough."

She shook her head. "No. We both need to see this through." She opened her hand and stared down at the ring.

Gideon slumped and then straightened again. He couldn't rush her. The heart and the mind often warred with each other. He'd have to continue to play the game—the one he promised V.J. they would plot out together.

What had he been thinking?

If Charisse's mind never got the message to her heart, Gideon wouldn't have the only broken heart.

He cleared his throat of the emotions stuck there. "Does this mean you're ready to put away the token of Vance's love for you?"

She nodded. "Yes. Vance's love lives on in my heart and in my son, not in these metals, no matter how precious they are to me."

"You know, someday the man who marries you should buy you a beautiful chain so that you can wear this ring around your lithe little neck."

"Why?" she asked.

"Without your marriage to Vance, the next man who marries you wouldn't receive the two most precious gifts in the world. This ring would remind the man you marry of the woman Vance helped you to become. He would also remember the little boy Vance left behind for him to raise into the man his father would want him to become." Gideon looked to the kid and the dog playing in the grass.

V.J. and Cletus ambled over to him.

"Why don't I pack away the coolers, and we can take a ride on one of the swan boats?" Gideon pointed.

V.J. stumbled back one step, then two. He shook his head, hard and fast. "No, Mommy. No." He threw himself into her arms.

Charisse wrapped him in an embrace. "It's okay, baby. We won't. We don't ever have to if you're not ready."

"Daddy," V.J. cried against her. "Daddy," his mournful wail filled the afternoon air.

"I don't understand." Gideon stood by helpless to calm the child.

"I want my daddy." V.J. choked.

Charisse laid a warm hand against Gideon's cheek. In her other hand she held up her wedding ring. "Those boats are this for him. V.J's daddy used to rent a paddleboat for us when we'd come here. I suspect V.J. doesn't want to cloud that memory with new ones we would make."

Gideon reached for V.J.

The boy turned into his embrace.

"I'm sorry," Gideon said. "That's one of your good memories, and I didn't mean to try to replace it." He hugged the sobbing boy to him. "Let it out, Veej."

"I want my daddy," the boy repeated. "I want my daddy."

Charisse turned away from them, but Gideon continued to hold her son. "It's okay to want him, Veej. There's nothing wrong with that desire." He pulled back from the hysterical little boy. "Look at me."

V.J. wiped his eyes with the back of his hand and stared up at him, his body trembling with hiccupping sobs.

Gideon wiped his own moist eyes. "I still want my dad, too. You'll always want him. The secret is not to bury him deep in your heart." He pointed toward the boats. "What do you remember about the boat rides with your dad?"

The kid wiped his nose against Gideon's shirt, and Gideon smiled. "Nice, Veej, real nice." He tousled the boy's blond hair. "Will you share your memories with me?"

V.J. cast an uncertain look in Charisse's direction. She smiled. "Do you know what I remember most?" He shook his head.

"How you and Daddy laughed so hard at me because I couldn't paddle once we got to the middle of the lake. You teased and teased me, and the two of you laughed. You have your daddy's laugh, V.J., and I love to hear it. It's one of my favorite memories of him, and you bring it alive for me every time I hear it."

"Daddy laughed so loud the swans honked at him, and that made you laugh. You teased Daddy about it, and Daddy hugged you. Then he hugged me, and he said, 'I love you guys very much,' and you told Daddy you weren't a guy." He stopped to take a quivering breath. "That made Daddy laugh again."

Gideon touched V.J.'s nose, and the boy threw his arms around him. "I love you, too, Judge Tabor."

"And I love you, Veej." Gideon held him. He put his mouth close to V.J.'s ear. "And I only want to be your 'nother dad," he whispered soft and low. "Not replace your daddy."

V.J. leaned away from him and then hugged him even tighter.

Cletus pushed his nose between them, and Gideon let the dog offer his sympathies as well.

"I can't wait for you and Mommy to share all your memories of your daddy with me." Gideon winked at

Charisse.

After all, without Vance Wellman, Charisse would not be the woman she was today.

And while he couldn't ethically look into the state's investigation of Vance Wellman's death, he knew someone who would take it on without a second thought.

Chapter Fourteen

Charisse bustled about the kitchen, happy to be cooking again for more than her and V.J. She stood back surveying all she'd done, making sure she hadn't left anything out. The roast was in the oven, baking with the carrots and potatoes, and the green beans simmered on the stove. The key lime pie chilled in the refrigerator. She wanted this meal perfect and for now all was well.

She ran up the stairs and changed into her jeans and top. "V.J.?" she called before starting downstairs.

No answer.

She went to his bedroom door. Closed. He never closed his door.

She turned the knob and pushed it open. V.J. sat on his bed with his back toward her. Vance's picture lay on the bed beside him. "Hey, baby, you okay?" she asked.

He turned with a beaming smile. "I'm fine, Mommy."

"What are you doing?" She moved inside and sat beside him. She fingered the picture of Vance.

Downstairs, she'd been preparing a meal for two men—one she thought she could love—and he was not her husband. While upstairs, V.J. was remembering his father.

"Do I look like Daddy, Mommy?"

She tore her gaze away from Vance's handsome face. "Yeah. Every bit of you looks like him. Why do you ask?"

"Because I've been forgetting what he looked like."

Charisse understood. At times, Vance's face was so clear, and at other times, all she could see were Gideon's green eyes, his brown hair, and his wonderful, loving smile.

"Do you think Daddy would mind my loving Judge Tabor the way I do?"

Charisse blinked at the connection in their thoughts. "How do you love Judge Tabor?"

He bit into his lower lip with his teeth.

"Let me guess. You love Judge Tabor almost as much as you love your daddy."

"Almost." He nodded. "But Daddy—"

"Daddy is wonderful, and Judge Tabor, he's—"

"He's great."

Charisse's heart echoed with the sentiment. "Here's what I think Daddy would say to you. Daddy would cross his arms over his chest, and he'd stare down at you, and he'd say, "Vance, Jr., you are to love with all your heart, and if someone breaks your heart, you're to love them twice as hard."

"That's what Daddy always said. That's what he told me when I got mad at my best friend in kindergarten. My friend broke my model plane Daddy made for me."

"I remember. And how did that work out?"

"Bobby's still my best friend."

Vance was a wise man. Charisse tweaked her son's nose. "Well, those are Daddy's rules, V.J. We need to listen to him. Love Judge Tabor with all your heart."

"Do you, Mommy?" he asked.

"Do I what?" She stood.

"Love Judge Tabor with all your heart?"

"Guess what?" She raised her brows.

"What?" He bounced up and down on his bed.

"I'm not telling you."

"Ah, Mommy." He faked a pout for her and then broke into a huge grin. "Judge Tabor can sing, can't he?"

"Yes, he can. Why?" She eyed him.

"Well, Daddy didn't sing too good."

"Too well," she corrected. "Your daddy had a voice that only God could love, but right now, he's probably singing in a choir—something no earthly music leader in his right mind would allow."

V.J. scooted to the edge of his bed. "I liked sitting between you and Judge Tabor at church today."

"I have to admit, it was nice sitting with him, too, baby, but Judge Tabor is still looking for a church. There's no guarantee he'll keep visiting with us."

"He will, Mommy. I know he will."

"Well, I hope so, too, but I don't want your feelings to get hurt if he doesn't stay. Our church is considered old fashioned. We sing old hymns, and right now we don't even have anyone who can play an instrument."

"Judge Tabor told me he liked it. He said he was going to come back."

Charisse hadn't heard Gideon's declaration, but her heart lifted at the thought.

"He said he liked to hear you singing out of tune."

"What?" She opened her mouth wide and feigned surprise. "He said that?"

"Yeah, he did." V.J. smiled and then shook his head. "No, he didn't."

"Why, you little rat." She tickled him. "So, I sing off key?"

"Yeah, you do." He squirmed in her hold.

"And for that remark, I'm going to sing louder tonight."

"No, Mommy, no." He pulled free and ran down the stairs.

Charisse caught up to him in the foyer. They both fell to the floor in a fit of hysterics.

"Knock, knock." Deacon said from the other side of the front door.

"Come in here and help me." Charisse called. "V.J.'s tormenting me." She tickled her little boy's tummy.

Deacon opened the door, and at the same time his mobile phone rang. "Young Judge Gideon," he answered.

Deacon's face lost its color before he turned away. "Are you okay? Sit tight. I'll be right there. A little too late. Yes, I'll tell her." He clicked off the call.

Charisse stood. "What is it, Judge Foster?"

"Gideon's had a car accident."

"Oh." Charisse gasped.

"He's all right, darlin' He said to make sure you knew. If you don't mind holding that dinner, we'll handle things and be back."

Charisse wanted to go with him, but her feet wouldn't move. "Is he off the road?"

"I don't know, darlin', but I'm sure he'll be careful."

Charisse gripped the older man's arm. "Please, please, tell him to stand far from the shoulder. Both of you."

Deacon patted her cheek. "I'll keep him safe for you."

As he closed the door, Charisse turned away. "Dear God, protect him. Please protect him."

"Mommy," V.J. tugged at her shirt. "I'm scared."

Charisse took his hand. "Then let's pray and ask God to look after Judge Tabor and Judge Foster."

Gideon knocked on Charisse's front door. She pulled it back, looking at him from head to foot. Deacon said news of his accident had shaken her, but he could see every line of worry on her face, brought out because of him. He touched Charisse's blonde strands and moved to allow Deacon to enter. "I stood on the other side of the guardrail." He winked. "I'll always do that if this ever happens again—just so you know."

"Judge Tabor, what happened?" V.J. ran to him.

"Nothing to be too concerned over, Veej. No one was injured. A driver changed lanes, and I was trapped in the center lane. I had nowhere to go." He looked back to Charisse. "It was either let him hit me or move into the other lane and hit someone else. I decided I'd rather take the hit."

Charisse's smile was plainly put in place for her son's benefit. "See, V.J., God answered our prayers."

And now he could trade the sports car in for a more practical vehicle—say a family car.

"Well, dinner is ready." Charisse led them into her dining room, and after Deacon offered a prayer of thanksgiving that Gideon felt deep inside his being, they dug in.

Gideon sat back in his seat. The woman he loved could cook, and by happenstance, she'd cooked his favorite meal. The roast beef was fall apart tender, and the potatoes and carrots baked to perfection. The green beans had just the right amount of bacon fat.

He loved the food at the Citrus, but he longed for the home-cooked meals he'd enjoyed in his youth.

Across the table from him, Charisse stared over his shoulder. He turned to follow her gaze.

The picture of Vance—still sitting in its glassless frame.

Was she continuing to struggle with the same issues or had something else arisen?

He needed to lighten the mood. He reached and picked a green bean from V.J.'s plate.

"Hey," the boy protested.

Gideon popped it in his mouth and chewed with exaggeration. "You better hurry, or I might grab some more." He held up his hand, ready to snatch another, glancing at Charisse.

At the head of the table, Deacon reached for Charisse's hand. "You okay, darlin'?"

"Mommy, tell Judge Tabor to stop eating my food," V.J. bantered.

Charisse brought her stare from the picture to

Deacon. "I'm sorry, what?"

"You seem a million miles away from us," Deacon told her.

"Judge Tabor's stealing my green beans." V.J. laughed.

"Well, hurry up and eat them, and he won't." She busied herself by straightening the napkin in her lap. "I'm fine, Judge Foster.

"Charisse?" Gideon tilted his head and offered her his best smile.

The look she returned was almost his undoing. He'd never seen such sadness in his life. She stood and motioned for the men and boy to stay put. "I made a special dessert." She gathered a few plates and took them with her, and then returned with a key lime pie and four dessert plates.

Gideon looked from the pie to her. Would happenstance have her actually fix the exact same dinner he'd loved in his youth complete with his favorite dessert? But how could she know?

Charisse sliced the pie, handing each of them a piece. "Gid." She didn't quite share eye contact with him.

She knew. He must have told her long ago. The little stinker remembered.

He smiled at V.J. and Deacon. "Are you looking forward to our reunion as much as I am?" he asked her as she sat.

Charisse's cheeks turned a deep rose under his gaze. "Not really. I'm sure the idiot I told you about is going to show up." The piece of dessert Charisse tried to get from plate to mouth with her trembling fork fell onto her lap.

She wiped it away with her napkin and stood. "Excuse me. This will stain my jeans." She ran into the kitchen.

"Yeah," Gideon said to the old man and the boy. "The idiot's going to show up," he leaned toward V.J, "and I'm either going to get a hug or a punch."

"When Mommy has parties, she always makes the punch with the sherbet in it. You'll like it, Judge Tabor." V.J. licked pie from his lips.

"Does your mommy hit like a girl?" Deacon asked the boy with a wink at Gideon.

"Yeah," V.J. said. "Oh." He looked to Gideon. "If she swings at you, though, you may want to duck."

"Excuse me, gentlemen." Gideon pushed away from the table.

Charisse stood at her kitchen counter just to the right of her sink. She ran her hand over and over a deep cut into the counter.

He touched her shoulder.

She turned around throwing her arms around his neck. "I'm sorry, Gideon. I'm so sorry. I promise. I won't be angry with you again."

"Oh, ho, that's a mighty big promise. I won't hold you to it. Just assure me you'll give me a chance to change your mind if I ever do something you disagree with again."

She nodded her head against him.

"And do me one favor, will you?"

"Whatever you want." She pulled away and ran her hand over the wet spot her tears had left on his shirt. Then she pulled her touch away.

He lifted her chin with his finger. "I hope if that idiot

shows up, you'll take the advice of a very wise man and live up to your name, Charisse. Give your idiot the same amount of forgiveness you've shown me today."

A beautiful smile lit her face. "Done!" She hugged him once again and left him standing there alone.

He wiped his brow. "I'll be reminding her of that promise, I'm sure," he said to himself before rejoining the others in the dining room.

Charisse pulled her dusty yearbook from the top of her closet and examined the picture of every female in her class. "Who are you?" she demanded. "If I knew, I could ask Libby if you've sent in your RSVP. If you intend to show up, I just won't. I'll wait for Gid to tell me he's going to live life happily ever after with someone else."

The realization hit her as soon as Deacon left to join Gideon at the accident site. She loved Gideon too much. He'd offered himself to her. All she had to do was ask him not to look for this mysterious woman, and he might have followed her home after the evening service to enjoy a nice family movie with V.J. Maybe they'd talk about future dates, make plans for tomorrow. He'd kiss her good night with a promise of more to come.

But no. She needed to give him the chance to see this other woman, to determine God's will in his life.

If he decided he loved the old friend more, what would she do? He declared his love for her and for V.J. He promised never to hurt her son, but to have him around and know he belonged to another woman—she couldn't live with that.

She looked closer at the yearbook and gave four girls the nod as definite possibilities. All had been cheerleaders, and they'd worshipped Gideon Tabor, All-American.

Her emotions moved inside her like bumper cars, the good, rational ones colliding with bad, irrational feelings that made her want to throw a fit. She sat in silence for several moments until the internal torment became too much for her.

"I hate this." She slammed the yearbook shut.

Her gaze fell upon her wedding photo, and tears pooled in her eyes. "Oh, I love you." She held her hands out as if Vance would appear from the small photo and become a part of her life again.

"I miss you." She swallowed down the sharp pain of loss and shook her head. "But I'm ready to move on, and I can't. Gideon doesn't know if he loves me enough." She covered her face with her hands.

She hadn't trusted God. She'd prayed, but not like she'd prayed for his safety this afternoon. She'd lacked faith when she asked God for Gideon's wholehearted love. If she would pray and believe, God would give her the desires of her heart—if the desires of her heart glorified Him.

She fell to her knees at the foot of her bed and bowed her head. "I loved Vance, Lord. You know I did. He was my world, and I accept that You allowed him to be taken away from us. I accept that Gideon had the best intentions with his verdict. I trust You." She sobbed. "I'm sorry for my anger with Vance before his death, with Gideon, and with You." She looked up. "And now, here I am with Gideon. The boy I wanted so long ago has become the man I want today." Again she bowed her head, resting her forehead on her hands folded in front of her. "Gideon told me to pray and to believe." Her voice strengthened. "Lord, You say that if it is Your will, You'll give us the desires of our heart. Please, dear God, make us the desire of Gideon's heart. Allow me to love him the way he deserves. Allow him to love my son and to raise V.J. up to love You.

"A faith like Gideon's will give V.J. a strong foundation to love You and to worship You." Charisse sat in silence for some time. Then she took a deep breath and smiled. "I believe. I believe. I do believe. Gideon will love me." She again looked heavenward. "Lord, direct Gideon's heart in my direction." She swallowed. "But whatever Your will, I'll rest in You."

She bowed her head in silent reverence to the God who'd never left her—even in her darkest moments when she thought she'd been alone. Then she opened her eyes. The smiling face staring back at her from the doorway brought her to her feet. "V.J." She stood, wiping the tears from her face. "What are you so happy about?"

"Judge Tabor was right."

"About what?" She studied him.

"He said you really loved Daddy, and you were just sad."

Why had he ever doubted? She sat and patted the bed. "And how did this conversation come about?"

V.J. shrugged and climbed up. With a bounce, he settled next to her.

Charisse resituated herself so that she could look at her son. "Judge Tabor's right. I do love your daddy. I always will. I didn't think you would doubt that."

"You told Daddy you hated him, Mommy. I heard you." V.J. looked up at her with expectant eyes.

"Oh." She ran her hand along the soft cotton of the bedspread. "Well, I'm sorry you heard me say that. I didn't mean it."

"I know. You've always loved him." V.J. moved to her. "But you love Judge Tabor, too."

Charisse laughed. She worked hard to make V.J. believe she and Gideon were only friends, and his eavesdropping on her prayers spilled her secret. "Yes, V.J., you figured it out. I do."

"With all your heart, the way Daddy said you're supposed to love someone?"

"Yes, baby, with all my heart, the way your daddy said."

"So, you're going to marry him?"

"Whoa. Sometimes when people love each other, it isn't enough. Judge Tabor and I have some things to figure out, and he may never ask me to marry him."

He studied her without saying anything.

"Whatever happens, Judge Tabor will always love you. Leave it to the grownups, okay?"

"Mommy, you won't punch him no matter what he does, will you?"

"What kind of question is that? When have I ever punched anyone, Veej?"

He straightened. "Only Judge Tabor can call me that."

"What?"

"You called me Veej. Judge Tabor calls me that."

She hadn't even realized she'd called him by the nickname Gideon gave to him, but his rejection of her use of it stung. "Oh, Judge Tabor can use it, but I can't?"

"Only Judge Tabor," V.J. nodded.

"Because you don't like it?"

"No, I like it."

"But not from me?" She swallowed down her pride and waited for him to answer.

He hesitated a moment and then shook his head. "No."

"Care to tell me why?" Like she needed something else to worry over tonight.

"Because V.J. stands for Vance, Jr., Daddy's name. Judge Tabor didn't know Daddy, so it's okay for him to call me Veej. I like it when he calls me that."

"I see." Charisse nodded. She should have known. V.J. was handling the past and the present the best way he knew how. "My big boy, can I call you that?

"Sure." He threw his arms around her neck. "I love you Mommy, and I'm not sad anymore. Are you?"

"I love you, Vance, Jr., and no, I'm not. I'm very happy."

V.J. sauntered to the bedroom door. "Mommy, do I have to keep calling him Judge Tabor?"

"What would you call him?"

V.J. pressed his lips together for a minute. Then he narrowed his eyes as if in thought. "For now, I'll call him Judge Tabor."

"For now?" She tilted her head.

Another big smile lit his face. "And when you marry him, I'll call him Dad."

"V.J. ..." She sputtered, but he ran toward his room.

Charisse stared at the yearbook. "I believe," she breathed. "God, I believe that You will order each of our steps."

Chapter Fifteen

It'd taken Gideon a few days to get up the nerve to ask his old friend John Turner for the favor. Now John stood before him with news he hadn't expected.

V.J's class had arrived an hour earlier. Charisse had volunteered to give them a tour of the courthouse and then to meet with the kids in his mediation room to answer any questions about her job. Their noisy voices and Charisse's call to order announced they must be nearing the end of her time with them.

Gideon pushed his chair back. It slammed against the credenza behind him. "You're kidding me. Tell me Delilah doesn't have that file." He ran his hand through his hair.

"What are you running out there, a daycare?"

Gideon glanced at his watch. "Back when I went to Veej's show-and-tell I invited his class on a field trip. His teacher took me up on it." He was due in court in fifteen minutes, and the kids would be sitting in on the arraignment docket. He'd pulled some strings to take court today and free up his weekend for the reunion.

The plan had been ingenious. He'd laughed about Delilah being forced into weekend duty, but that was before he realized he'd stirred up a hornet's nest. "Delilah checked out the Fullwell file? You're sure it was her?"

"Well, Crystal, yeah." John stood. "She's had it too

long. I asked the clerk's office to notify me when she returns it. I'll look it over to see if there's anything the state might have missed, but I can't promise you anything."

"How do you think Delilah put it together?" Gideon paced. "And what could she hope to gain?"

John touched the back of the seat he'd vacated. "She's a very astute woman, Gideon. If Charisse gave her a slight hint of a court case, Dee would be all over it."

"If she's so perceptive, tell me why she hasn't seen your interest in her."

"Yeah, right. That woman would make a terminator scream for mercy." John moved toward the door. "My advice to you is to play dumb. She's not going to hurt you. One of the reasons she hasn't noticed me is because she's tuned into you."

"I've told her that's not going to happen."

John stepped back toward him. "Tell me you left her some dignity."

Gideon studied his friend. He owed John the truth. "She tried very hard to act as if I had, but I think it shook her."

A light knock sounded at his door before John could respond.

"Come in," Gideon called.

Charisse entered. "V.J.'s class is all yours, boss. Hello, Mr. Turner, how are you?"

John moved toward the door. "I'm fine, Charisse, and please feel free to call me John. I don't have a complex like the good judge over there." He turned back to Gideon. "I'll let you know what I find out and what I can do to help."

Gideon nodded. "Thanks."

"Hi, Judge Tabor." V.J. leaned in the door as John walked out.

"Hey, Veej. Be with you and your class in a few minutes."

Charisse spoke to her son and then closed the door. "I've answered their many questions. Mrs. Carlyle told me you provided them with some interesting information about court procedure and law."

Gideon laughed. "Did I forget to tell you? Your old friend Judge Kenley kindly donated the materials he said *you* prepared for his study."

Charisse shook her head. "You can forget to tell me you contacted him, but you remembered his name and the fact I even worked with him on the project, and the only time we've spoken about this was during my interview."

"I have a mind like a steel trap. Often, though, it rusts shut."

"Well, like I said, we had a question-and-answer session, and I also cautioned them on how they should behave in your courtroom. They belong to you now, and I'm going back to work." She opened the door.

"Four requests," he said and smiled as she turned back toward him, shutting the door.

"Only four?"

"I have several cases I need copied, and Delilah has asked if you could do some research on the issue of special equity. Since she's a little angry with me, I told her I'd ask. Do you have time?"

"Gladly, so long as you deal with the kids."

"That brings me to my third request."

"Uh-oh." She closed her eyes.

"Can you call Fratelli's and remind them the troops will be marching down the street around eleven thirty."

"Fratelli's?"

"Yeah, I called them last week. I'm treating the kids to pizza."

"I'll let them know." She stood with her hands on her hips. "And what else?"

"I'm not leading the battalion alone."

She dropped her hands and stared at him. "I have too much to do. I can't go. I'll call Judge Foster, and Mrs. Carlyle will be with you."

"Deacon's welcome to come, but I'm not facing Mrs. Carlyle without her favorite punching bag in front of me."

"For your information, Mrs. Carlyle and I kissed and made up. She was so bowled over by your kindness in providing her the materials for the class, she apologized to me. So there." She stuck her tongue out at him.

He moved around his desk and stood in front of her. "Indulge me in a fifth request?"

"Yes," her blue eyes stared up at him.

"Will you and V.J. have dinner with me tonight?" She smiled. "We'd love to."

"Because you know tomorrow, at the reunion, I'm looking up my old flame."

Her smile vanished. "Let's not talk about that now. You have court. I have work." She rushed from his office.

Gideon fought to keep from going after her, telling her the truth, but his plans were almost in place. He just needed one other inside person, and the Lord had not revealed that person to him yet. He went to the door leading into the courtroom. "Bill," he motioned to his bailiff.

Bill stepped into the office and then out into the reception area with Gideon.

"Good morning, ladies and gentleman." Gideon grabbed the children's attention. "Who's ready for a little court action?"

"Me!" A chorus rang out.

"It's very important you remember Mrs. Wellman's instructions on how to act in court." He motioned to Bill. "This is Bailiff Bill, and he is responsible for keeping order in my courtroom. He doesn't tolerate the least bit of noise. You'll want to stay on Bailiff Bill's good side."

The tower of a man stood in silence, his arms across his chest. Children snapped to attention.

"He's got a gun," an awed child said.

"Judge Tabor won't let him shoot us."

Gideon smiled at the boy's confidence in him. "Okay, Bailiff Bill, lead the way." Gideon slipped back into his office to await Bill's summons into the courtroom.

Charisse finally had a chance to get to the copier room. Staff had been utilizing it all morning. Now, after clearing two paper jams, she had the last set of papers in the document feeder. She pushed the green button with a sense of accomplishment.

Judge Foster entered. "Are you expectin' someone to

join you for lunch?"

She turned to him. "I'm sorry, Judge Foster. No, I'm having lunch with Gideon and the kids. Why?"

"Well, you need to take a break right now."

She couldn't do that. The court administrator had asked her for a report by five o'clock, and she still needed to provide research for Delilah. She could tell Gideon about the report and ask for a reprieve from Delilah's work, but Delilah's behavior of late had been very good— at least for the vindictive judge. Charisse didn't want to push the red button and release the nuclear weapon.

"Charisse, girl, are you listenin' to me?" The judge waved his hand in front of her.

"I'm sorry, what?" Charisse blinked from her thoughts.

"There's a young gal out there, and she needs rescuin'." His accent seemed exaggerated by his anxiousness. "You better come quickly before that rabbit toter gets her fangs in her."

"What are you talkin'—talking about?"

"You ain't heard tell of a rabbit toter? They're someone so mean and ugly a dog won't even play with them unless they're carryin' a rabbit."

Charisse laughed. She picked up and stapled her copies before following Judge Foster down the hall, stopping short as she saw the prey within reach of the rabbit toter's fangs.

Judge Foster urged her on with the nod of his head, and Charisse shot him an irate glare.

"There she is now." Delilah's smile dripped venom.

"Charisse." Libby stood. She brushed at the hair that

fell into her face and moved closer to Charisse. "I've just been talking with Judge James."

"I'm glad to see you, although I think it means your mother is in the hospital." Charisse forced herself closer to the scene and wrapped her friend in a hug. "Have you met Judge Foster?"

"No, I haven't."

"It's a delight." The judge came forward.

"I never thought I'd meet one judge, let alone two." Libby blushed. She turned and looked at the name plate on Gideon's door.

Charisse tried to place a smile on her face and into her words. "What brings you here?"

"Oh." Libby pushed her big round glasses up on her nose. "We made it as long as we could, but Momma had some complications. She's in the hospital here. I needed a little break and decided to come by and see you."

And Lord, here I am with no time at all to offer her after all the smiles she's put on my face, the advice she's given, and the prayers she's lifted to You on my behalf.

"Libby, I'd love to join you for lunch, but—"

"Quarterly reports are due, and Charisse volunteered some important research for me. On top of all that, she has a courtroom full of kids to babysit." Delilah licked her lips, the false gleam of innocence shining so brightly Charisse winced.

"Judge Tabor invited V.J.'s class here today, and he's taking them to lunch at Fratelli's. Would you like to join us?"

"No, I wouldn't feel comfortable barging in on such a big party."

"I'm going out. Would you care to join me?" Delilah offered.

Judge Foster made a gesture with his hands urging Charisse back into the conversation.

"Charisse, would you mind, since you're so busy?" Libby asked.

Am I to sacrifice her to Delilah— Libby in the Lions' den?

Daniel prevailed because the Lord shut the lions' mouths.

I'd rather her be thrown to the real lions, Lord.

Have a little faith, Charisse. It's something you've lacked lately. You've gotten into a real bind all by yourself. Care to accept My help?

Why was she thinking like this? Charisse shrugged at the conversation in her head.

"It's settled then." Libby mistook Charisse's action for an acceptance of her plans.

"I'll get my purse." Delilah disappeared into her office.

"Libby, be careful."

"Have a little faith in me, okay?" Libby smiled, and Charisse blinked at the similarity in her thoughts and Libby's spoken words.

"What hospital is your mom in?"

"Orlando Regional, Room 503."

"I'll visit with her after work. You'll be there, right?"

Libby nodded. "But don't feel obligated."

Charisse smiled. "I love visiting with you and your mother."

Delilah stepped out of her office. She stood, arms at

her side, a smile in place. Charisse had never known her to look so patient.

"I'll see you tonight then." Libby waved.

"Rabbit toter," Judge Foster muttered.

Delilah turned sharply, glared at him, and then offered her full attention to her victim.

"Some friend I am." Charisse walked into her office.

Gideon leaned back in his chair and stretched. The children were gone, having enjoyed a delightful lunch at the Italian diner around the corner. Mrs. Carlyle had begged Gideon not to encourage a food-eating contest. He'd complied, but the burping contest was fun, and when V.J. won by a vote of his classmates, the horror on Charisse's face had been priceless.

Through his open door, Gideon caught a glimpse of the woman standing in the corridor with Charisse. He leaned to the side to get a better look. The woman turned toward him. Her eyes registered surprise before she pushed her oversized glasses up on her face and turned away too quickly. Libby—Libby Overstreet.

God had provided an inside person after all.

"I'll see you later, Charisse," Libby said.

Gideon hustled to the door in his chambers that led into his courtroom. If he moved fast enough he could intercept Libby outside the elevator.

"You." Charisse walked into his office without a knock. "You are incorrigible, Gideon Tabor."

Gideon held to the door. "Give me a minute."

Charisse stared at him. "Is everything okay?"

"Yeah, I need to take care of something." He bounced up and down. He'd rather stay in Charisse's delightful company, but he needed an ally. Libby was the perfect one.

"The bathroom's that way." She pointed and laughed as she left.

Funny. He'd have laughed if he had the time.

Gideon ran through his empty courtroom and into the hall. "Psst." He motioned to Libby who stood waiting for the elevator.

Libby turned toward him and pointed at herself.

"Yeah, Libby, you. Can I see you for a minute?"

"You remember me?" She took a tentative step toward him.

The elevator dinged and the door opened. Gideon ran to it, pulling a wide-eyed Libby inside. "Yeah, I do."

Libby glared at him. "Shame on you for not telling her."

"Shame on me?" Gideon leaned back. "For not telling her what?"

"Gideon Tabor, you have something you need to tell Charisse." She placed her hands on her hips. "Shame on you."

"What do I need to say to her?" The door opened on the second floor, and Gideon waved the group of people away. He pushed the button, and the door closed. "Libby, tell me, what you think I'm keeping from Charisse?"

Libby shook her finger at him. "This has been torture for her. She told me you know about Vance's trial, but you're playing games with her, and I don't like it one bit."

His ally, the one he needed to assure he could pull everything off without a pitch, she was now his foe, and he didn't know why.

The elevator door opened, and he followed Libby into the lobby. Who would have thought the petite, quirky gal from high school would have so much spunk and be such a fierce defender of Charisse? For that, she had Gideon's undying gratitude, even if she was a tad furious with him. "Tell me, Libby. Why are you angry with me?"

"Because, you big oaf, you've always been in love with her, and you're teasing her about this mysterious woman you're looking to find at the reunion. You and I both know that girl has always been Charisse. You've loved her forever, and don't tell me you haven't."

So Charisse had confided in her little buddy, who just told him everything he needed to know. He picked up Libby and twirled her around. "Libby, you're right, and V.J. and I have a plan. We need a helper. Care to join us in the conspiracy?"

"On one condition." She swooned as he put her down. He reached out to steady her. She pulled from him and straightened her skirt and top.

"Anything." He waited.

"You never let her know I had any part in this." She reached in her purse and pulled out a card, thrusting it toward him. A business card with a Bible verse.

He took it from her. "How'd you know I loved Charisse in high school? She apparently never had a clue."

Libby's eyes grew large behind her glasses. "Duh! It was written all over your big dumb face, and I was in your trigonometry class. You did pretty well in there, but you sure acted all stupid when you wanted Charisse to tutor you." She started away.

Gideon laughed. "Libby?"

Libby turned back to him.

Gideon held up the card. "Thank you for helping us."

"I love Charisse and V.J. I loved Vance." She smiled. "And Gideon, I have always had a soft spot in my heart for you, especially because I knew what you missed out on when you didn't get a chance to show Charisse how much you loved her."

Gideon leaned against the doorframe to Charisse's office, soaking in her beauty while she pecked away on her keyboard. Her blonde hair framed her face, cascading over her shoulders. Her teeth bit into her lower lip as she continued to work. "So, you were yelling at me before I made an exit. What did I do wrong?" He feigned innocence.

"You put V.J. up to that little display of ill manners. Of all things."

Gideon lifted his arms. "Me? Your son suggested the contest." Of course, he'd planted the seed in his mind the night before when they spoke on the phone, but who was telling?

"I suppose having his teacher call me about that type of behavior is better than having her insinuate I'm an unfit mother."

Soon, if Gideon had his way, the teacher could call

him anything she wanted, as long as she called him V.J.'s dad.

"Can I see you for a minute?" Delilah came to the door.

Gideon quirked his eyebrows at Charisse. Since when had Delilah ever politely asked for his attention? "Sure, Dee. Let's go in my office. Charisse, tonight six thirty? I'll pick you and Veej up at your place."

Charisse nodded. "As long as we're home by nine. I have to be in Titusville early tomorrow."

He nodded and followed Delilah toward his office. He left the door open, but when Delilah entered she closed it. He sat behind his desk, and she took the chair in front of him.

"Something wrong?" he asked.

She shook her head and ran a finger under her eyes.

Tears? This wasn't like Delilah James at all.

Gideon's stomach churned. The milk he had at lunch would turn to butter before too long.

"A friend of Charisse's stopped by to have lunch with her today."

"Libby Overstreet. She's something else."

"I had lunch with her instead." Delilah eyed him.

"I hope you didn't do it to cause trouble."

Delilah stared at him and then shook her head. "Of course I did it to cause trouble, but I didn't get very far."

Honesty. He hadn't expected it. Gideon leaned back in his chair. "What's going on?"

"Like I said, I had lunch with Libby."

How in the world did Charisse allow that to happen? "I'm not sure I like where this is heading."

Delilah again swiped at her eyes. Gideon reached for the Kleenex on the credenza behind him and handed her one. Libby must have fired back for Delilah to have such a reaction. He couldn't wait to learn the identity of Delilah's Kryptonite.

"In all fairness, I did ask her to lunch so I could at least make Charisse uncomfortable."

Charisse did seem a little preoccupied at Fratelli's until the burping contest. Then she'd done her best to admonish V.J. without breaking into laughter.

"I started asking questions about Charisse and her husband, and that little spitfire chewed me up and spit me out."

Gideon roared with laughter but stopped when Delilah showed no amusement. "Please tell me you didn't hurt Libby."

"You must not know that woman too well." Now, a smile broke through Delilah's tears. "She told me she and Charisse had figured out my game, and she didn't appreciate being used to hurt her best friend."

"I'm at a loss. What did you do to hurt Charisse?"

"I may have lied and said something unkind about the way she used to look." She straightened in her seat as if preparing for battle.

"And what might you have said about the way she looked?"

"Promise me you'll stay on that side of the desk."

"What did you say, Dee?"

She hid her face behind the Kleenex. "I told her you called her obese."

Gideon held to the arms of the chair, his hands biting

into the leather.

"Don't worry. Libby set me straight, and she told me they figured out I'd found her picture on your high school's reunion website. Charisse knows you'd never say anything so cruel."

"Especially since it's a lie. Charisse has always been beautiful and wow. Good for Libby." She'd taken on two circuit court judges in one day, and all for her friend.

"Then like a fortune teller, Libby began to tell me things about myself I thought no one knew."

She had his attention. "Such as?" Gideon waited, breath held.

"She told me I'm not as confident as I want everyone to think. She said I'm afraid people aren't going to like me, so I don't give them a chance." Delilah dabbed at her eyes with the Kleenex. "She said I hurt people because I'm afraid they're going to hurt me first."

"And all that's true?" Gideon asked her.

Delilah smirked. "What do you think? You've said it, but not as bluntly as Libby."

"Did she tell you where she majored in psychology?" Gideon teased.

Delilah pinched her lips together and shook her head at him. "Don't, Gideon. Don't make light of this. It's hard for me."

He pushed from his chair. He moved to stand in front of her, leaning against the desk. "I'm sorry. Go on. I'm listening."

"Libby did something no one else has ever done, even you." She folded and unfolded the Kleenex.

Gideon retrieved another one. Handing it to her, he

again used the desk as a seat, crossing his feet at the ankles. "What'd she do?"

"She asked me why."

Gideon tilted his head. "Why what?"

"Why I feel the way I do." She jumped to her feet and paced away from him. "And I did something I'd never done. I told someone."

"Are you up to telling someone else who really cares?"

Delilah turned from him for a moment. Her shoulders shook. Finally, she straightened and turned to him. "My father left home when I was very young. My mother didn't handle it well. She dumped me on my grandmother's doorstep, and to dear Grandma, I was a burden. I don't think the woman ever said a kind word to me." Delilah hiccupped and waved her hand in the air as if dismissing the past. "That's just me trying to give excuses." She managed a short laugh. "At least that's what Libby says. 'We all have pasts,' she said. 'It's what we do with them that counts.'"

"Wisdom," Gideon remarked.

She took her seat once again. "Well, I learned in high school that if I walked taller than anyone, worked harder than anyone, dressed sharper than anyone, and acted as if I was better than everyone, people believed it."

He'd believed it.

"But the more I built myself up, the more I had to tear everyone down, and I had to keep everyone at a distance so they couldn't figure out the truth."

Libby Overstreet had gotten this out of Delilah in one hour, and Gideon had known her for several years.

Gideon placed his hand in his pocket and fingered the card holding Libby's number. He sure wouldn't cross that woman. No way. "How did Libby get under your skin like this?"

"She told me there was someone who knew everything about me, and that nothing had ever occurred in my life that took Him by surprise."

Gideon raised his brows, waiting.

Delilah laughed again, a genuine laugh. "Libby actually carries a small Bible with her in her purse, and she pulled it out. She showed me how well God knows me. She said that she'd been praying for a time to meet me, and she wasn't surprised Charisse was too busy to have lunch with her today."

"And?"

"Gideon, she introduced me to a Father who has always loved me and will never leave me."

"And?"

"And I asked Him to be my Father." Delilah buried her face into her hands.

"Dee, that's wonderful." Gideon bent down in front of her. "That's the most wonderful news I've heard in a long time."

She searched his face. "But where do I go from here? Libby said I needed to tell someone I trust. Now that I've told you, what's next?"

Gideon touched her hand. "Tell Charisse."

Delilah coughed. "Why would she care?"

Gideon smiled up at her. "She's probably going to think you're up to something, especially if you do it in your typical fashion, but she will care, and she's been a

Christian a lot longer than me, and she's a female, and she's ..." He looked toward his closed office door. "Delilah, Charisse is the woman I have always loved. I know her capacity for kindness and warmth. You have something in common. I know how deeply her father's abandonment hurt her."

Delilah blew her nose.

"But do me a favor, will you?" he asked. "Don't change. I mean, yeah, change the bad habits, realize you are loved, and let down your guard a little bit. You're a very special person. There's no one quite as bodacious as you. If you allow Christ to use your personality, let him smooth the rough edges, you'll be unstoppable."

She stood again.

"And Dee?" He stood. "That file you had Crystal check out, please don't hurt Charisse with it."

Delilah took a deep breath and let it out slowly. "Truth?"

"What have you done?"

"It's not what I've done, but it's what I haven't done." Delilah shook her head as if shaking off something she didn't want to deal with. "Don't worry about it. I'll handle it. Libby's mom's in the hospital. Libby asked me to come by this evening for a visit. Charisse said she was visiting her, too. I'll talk to her then." Delilah touched his face with the palm of her hand. "Charisse Wellman is a lucky woman. I'll never forget that you tried to open this door of wondrous freedom, and I slammed it in your face."

"God's in the details, Delilah, and he's always full of surprises. Who knew I'd ever see Charisse again, and that she'd bring a little spitfire to introduce you to our Lord?"

FAY LAMB

Chapter Sixteen

Charisse walked the sterile corridor checking the numbers on each door. Downtown traffic had been heavy, and she'd missed a turn to get into the hospital parking lot. Now, she needed to make her visit and get to V.J.'s after-school daycare before they charged her extra. She also didn't want Gid to have to wait for her.

She found Room 503, stopped, straightened her skirt, and lowered her head, saying a prayer that the Lord would allow her to repair the damage Delilah surely caused.

She rapped on the door and stepped inside. "Oh." She stopped.

Her nemesis sat in a chair by Madge Overstreet's bedside. Delilah stood and eyed her up and down. A smile slithered across Delilah's face. A new tactic ... maybe. It worked. Charisse was thoroughly thrown off guard.

She tightened her fist. This was the last straw. She would not let Delilah bully her one more moment.

Delilah stepped toward Charisse. "Well, Madge, I see you have another visitor. I won't monopolize your time."

"Charisse." Alerted to her visit, Libby jumped from her chair and linked her arm in hers. "Delilah, don't rush off. Momma, Charisse is here."

Charisse skirted Delilah and moved to the bed. She liked to remember Mrs. Overstreet as she appeared when Charisse was in third grade: a tall, proud, impeccably dressed woman holding a tray of cupcakes. Instead, she sorrowed over the shell of the woman Mrs. Overstreet now conveyed.

"Charisse." Mrs. Overstreet nodded. "It's so nice to have all this company. It's usually just Libby and me." She adjusted the oxygen tube lying against her nose.

"Well, I'll let Charisse visit." Delilah pushed toward her exit.

Charisse cast a glare she hoped spoke volumes.

"I'll wait outside, Charisse. I do want to talk to you." Delilah adjusted her purse strap.

Charisse shook her head. "I'll be a while, and I have plans." No use pretending they were friends.

"I'll wait." Delilah insisted and then walked out.

Charisse turned to her friend. "Anything she told you, don't give it a second thought."

Libby shook her head. "Delilah has a lot to say to you."

"I bet she does," Charisse muttered. "Mrs. Overstreet, are they treating you well?"

"Call me Madge. You're not a teenager any longer." Madge struggled to sit up.

Libby rushed to her aid. She fluffed the pillow and assured her mother's comfort.

"Libby fills me in on the work you girls are doing getting ready for the reunion." Madge ran a hand through her salt and pepper hair.

"Libby is the backbone of the committee."

Madge smiled. "Libby can do anything she puts her mind to do. She should be far away from here, but she stayed to take care of me."

"And I admire her for her decision." Charisse gave Libby a reassuring smile.

"Momma, there's nowhere else I want to be." Libby sat on the bed.

"You should be married with children or at least opening that flower shop or nursery we've always dreamed about and not tending an old woman who should have met the Lord long ago."

"Madge," Charisse scolded, "if you were meant to be with the Lord long ago, you'd be before Him now."

Madge laughed and coughed. "That's so true."

Charisse and Libby traveled Memory Road with Madge for several minutes, but when the older woman's eyes drooped, Charisse's intuition told her it was time to leave. Another glance at the precious woman revealed she had drifted off to sleep.

"It's the medication," Libby explained.

"I'll try to get back to see her, and when she goes home, I'll make it a point to stop by with V.J."

"Thanks so much." Libby walked her to the door.

Charisse embraced her friend and held her close for a long moment. "You're wonderful." She pulled back and stared into Libby's moist eyes. "Thanks for being my friend."

Libby started to speak but tears choked her voice, and she remained silent. How many lonely nights had Libby spent in these cold, sterile hospital rooms tending to her mother? Charisse's heart wrenched at the sudden realization.

She placed a hand against Libby's cheek. "You've done this for so long on your own. I'm so sorry I never noticed."

"Charisse, you've gone through a lot in the last year."

"We'll make it, won't we?"

"I think we will. No matter what happens, we'll get through this. The Lord has blessed me with two friends close by, one old and one new."

Charisse closed her eyes. "You're not talking about Delilah?" Libby couldn't be that gullible. Sure she found good in everyone, but with Delilah, she'd have had to dig deep.

"Shh." Libby placed her finger to her lips. "I'll see you tomorrow. I'll be a little late for the decorating, but I'll be there. I gave Karen the key to my house. Everything we'll need is in the garage."

"Is your mother being released?"

Libby shook her head and studied the tile on the floor. "No, she's not strong enough."

"You can get away?"

"By way of a miracle, yes I can." Libby smiled.

Charisse headed to the elevators. Maybe she could get out without a scene with the Honorable Delilah James. She needed to pick up V.J. and get home before Gideon arrived to take them to dinner.

"Sneaking off without me?" Delilah stepped from behind and punched the elevator's down button.

"Why don't you leave me alone?" Charisse stared straight ahead.

"If you didn't have to, you wouldn't give me the time of day, would you?"

"No, Judge James, I wouldn't." The empty elevator opened, and Charisse hurried inside. Delilah joined her.

"Fair enough. I understand why you feel this way about me."

The door closed, and Charisse placed her hands on her hips. She started to speak but shook her head instead.

"Say what you have to say," Delilah urged.

"You wouldn't want to hear it."

"Start by telling me I've been a thorn in your side since day one. I'm mean and underhanded. I tried to push you into complaining to the court administrator so he'd think you're a troublemaker and fire you. I garnered intel from Libby to use against you."

The elevator released her from her confines, and Charisse moved away from Delilah at a fast pace.

"Charisse!"

People in the lobby turned to stare.

Charisse kept moving.

"Stop, Charisse."

No way. She didn't have to put up with Delilah on her own time.

"Please, Charisse."

A request—politely made by the rudest woman Charisse had ever known? She stopped, and without warning, Delilah clasped her hand around Charisse's forearm, her nails digging into Charisse's skin as she propelled her toward the cafeteria. Charisse jerked from Delilah's grip only to be handed a tray on which the judge placed two pieces of carrot cake before retrieving forks and napkins.

Tray in hand, Charisse looked for a place to set it down before leaving. "Don't even think about it," Delilah said, with no hint of the vulnerability she'd exhibited in her plea for Charisse to remain. Yet, she smiled. "Nothing stands between me and my carrot cake. You aren't leaving with that tray." She motioned Charisse to follow her. The woman filled two cups with coffee and added them to Charisse's burden. Like a dutiful servant, Charisse followed Delilah through the line where Delilah paid and then into the dining room. "You won't want to miss what's coming for the world." Delilah took the desserts and coffees from the tray and placed them on the table. She then lifted the tray from Charisse's hand and set it aside "Sit."

Charisse shook her head and folded her arms over her chest.

Delilah scooted into the booth. "Good. Stand there." She shrugged. "Let me continue the recourse of why life has been so terrible for poor little Charisse at the hands of Delilah James."

"You've gotten it right so far."

"Where was I? Oh, yes, the discovery I used against you."

"You found my picture from the school website and made it seem as if Gideon—"

Delilah waved Charisse's comment away. "Then, I find out …" she stopped.

"Go ahead." Charisse's level of anger matched her voice.

Delilah sank a fork into the carrot cake and took a

bite. "This is delicious. Sit. Eat."

"Finish what you were going to say, Judge James."

"Why? So you can blast me for it?"

"You found out what?" Charisse lowered her voice.

"You know good and well what I found out." Delilah stabbed the cake again and took another bite.

Charisse tapped the toe of her shoe against the cafeteria's tile floor. "What was it you called me? Oh, yeah, a stalker."

"No, I actually attributed Gideon to that saying, but there you go. Another lie to add to your list. He never said a thing like that about you." The judge wiped her mouth with her napkin.

"You also said I was obese."

"Well, you were."

"Just because something's true doesn't mean you have to use it to hurt someone. Overweight people can't always help it."

"But you could. Look at you today. You don't even work out, do you? In order to eat like this, I have to spend two hours every day at the gym."

"I didn't diet to lose the weight. Losing your husband does something to your appetite."

Delilah waved her fork. "Add that to my list of faults. I was insensitive. I used offensive language about your weight. I didn't care to know you lost a husband until I thought I could use it as leverage. I didn't like your son. Oh, and I went to Gideon's house to demand he fire you."

"You what?"

"Don't worry. He wouldn't hear of firing his wonderful law clerk."

"I just do the job God gave me."

"To Giddy you are the most wonderful creation in the universe." Delilah took another bite of her cake, but not so enthusiastically. When she reached for her coffee cup, her hand trembled. Delilah left the cup sitting on the table.

Charisse stared at Delilah for a moment. Why hadn't she noticed the pain in the woman's eyes, so deep that in discovering it, Charisse lost the air in her lungs? She sat hard in the chair and reached to cover Delilah's hand with hers. "You love him. That's what all this is about."

"Of course, I love him. I have loved him since the day the big galoot walked into the courthouse like a little boy visiting Disney World. Mr. Tabor goes to the Orange County Legal System to right all the injustices in our fair city."

Charisse smiled at the picture Delilah painted with her words.

Delilah's piercing stare caused Charisse to look away. "I never had a chance with him"

Charisse closed her eyes. Despite their differences, their love for Gideon was something they shared. She fought against trembling lips as she gave Delilah her attention. "We both may love him, but the truth is Gideon isn't quite sure what he wants. He's in love with a girl from his past."

Delilah stared at her, mouth open. Then she gave an uncharacteristic giggle. "You are a trip, Charisse Wellman, and Gideon, he's a mess. Will that man ever …?" Again, she waved the fork. "No, he's never going to grow up. You're welcome to him. I want a man, not a kid in a man's body, no matter how well built or gorgeous he is."

"Neither one of us has a chance." And she loved the kid inside Gideon. Who wouldn't?

Delilah wiped her eyes, moist from the tears that formed with her laughter.

"So, you wasted your time with all the trouble you caused me." Charisse stood and looked down at the smiling woman.

"That's not what Libby told me."

The rage began to build like a rising wave. She gripped the edge of the table to keep her hand from flying against Delilah's unsuspecting face. No matter the depth of Delilah's pain, Charisse wouldn't let her take it out on Libby. All the while she prayed for God to allow her to live up to her name. *Be gracious.*

Charisse took a deep breath. "Libby doesn't need your petty games. She's going through so much."

"Charisse, please sit down and eat."

"My son is still in after-school care, and I'm paying an extra two dollars an hour after six thirty." Charisse looked at her watch. "That's in ten minutes." And Gideon would be waiting.

"You're not going to make it in time anyway. Don't you want to hear about my conversation with Libby and why she says all this destructive behavior hasn't been a waste of time, at least for me?"

"As far as I'm concerned, this is the last conversation I ever want to have with you." So much for being gracious to a hurting woman. Charisse sat again and pulled the extra carrot cake in her direction. No use letting it go to Delilah's waist.

"Libby introduced me to another friend of yours, a mutual friend of Gideon's as well. Gideon tried to introduce me to Him once, and I said I had no interest."

Charisse put down her fork.

"When Libby made the introduction, my heart opened wide. I realized what I missed out on by not listening to Gideon and not seeing what it was that helped you endure all the trouble I sent your way."

"Delilah," Charisse sounded a warning whisper. "No one should take God's love lightly."

"I met Jesus today while having lunch with Libby." Delilah narrowed her gaze at Charisse as if daring her to contradict her. "Libby seemed to think God allowed me to make trouble for you so I could see the strength you have in Him." Delilah stretched her napkin across her lap. She peered over the top of Charisse's head for a second before looking her straight in the eyes. "Still, I'm sorry for all the trouble I've caused."

Charisse studied at the woman for a very long time, the tide of anger ebbing. Delilah belonged to God. She realized the truth in much the same way God's children recognize each other in a crowd—having never met before. And this Delilah—Charisse had never met.

Charisse swiped at the tears that rolled down her cheek.

Delilah leaned forward, planted her elbow on the table, and cupped her chin in her hand. She stared across at Charisse. "Is that waterfall for me?"

Charisse reached for a napkin and, wiping her face, hid behind the paper for several seconds. "I don't know.

They're tears of happiness either for you or for me. Jesus will change your heart, Delilah, if you let Him. For that, I'm very grateful. Does Gideon know?"

She nodded. "I think the news left him speechless. He mentioned a wonderful church for me to attend, said he's gone the last two weeks, and he really enjoys it."

The Lord was surely trying her. If Gideon's long lost love decided to marry him, would he bring her to church, too?

They ate in silence and when Charisse stood, Delilah joined her. "I have something else I need to share with you."

Charisse braced for whatever Delilah would throw her way.

"I had the clerk's office send me the Carson Fullwell file. You've been to law school. How did you handle Gideon's directed verdict? They don't happen all the time."

Charisse touched her hand to her chest. Delilah had Charisse right where she'd always wanted her. What would the judge do with the information now? "I'm still dealing with it, but Gideon said he had a good reason, and I believe him."

"He was right, you know."

Charisse straightened. "How do you know that?"

Delilah looked at her watch. "Can we meet later? I promised Mrs. Overstreet I'd play Canasta with her while I stay with her tomorrow. Haven't played the game in years. I need to buy a how-to book. Do you play?"

Charisse blinked at the change in subject. "Please tell me." Desperation clung to her like humidity against her skin, threatening to overwhelm her.

"I know you have a date with Wonder Judge. Why don't you tell him I'd like to speak to both of you about the case?"

"When?"

"Later. I'll be happy to come to your place or to meet you somewhere?"

Charisse rattled off her address and phone number while Delilah plinked it into her phone. "We should be home by nine fifteen." She reached for Delilah's hand. "This isn't another way to hurt me, is it?"

Delilah patted her hand as if Charisse were a small child needing comfort. "If it was, do you think I'd invite Gideon? He would end my life if I injured the lo—his little law clerk." She pulled from Charisse's touch.

"Did you say you're staying with Madge tomorrow?"

"Yeah, we're kicking Libby out so she can join you at the reunion, and we're spending the afternoon together." Delilah walked ahead of her, and Charisse followed shaking her head.

As they reached the hospital door, Delilah turned back. "*Our* friend, Libby, is a wall of protection for you. She made it clear she didn't like me twisting her words to hurt you."

"I don't like it either."

"Didn't think you did. That's why it was so much fun." Delilah stopped at the edge of the sidewalk. "I learned two truths today."

"Oh, yeah. Care to share?"

"I'm not perfect."

"And?"

"Neither are you." Delilah smirked and strolled away with barely a wave.

Charisse shook her head. Delilah would always be a challenge, no matter what.

Once inside her car, Charisse dialed Gideon. "Hi, I'm going to be late." She put the key into the ignition.

"You okay?" he asked her.

"I—Delilah …"

"That's good news. You don't sound too happy. What's wrong?"

"She told me she has some news about Vance's case."

"I repeat, you okay?"

"She's coming to my house tonight."

"So dinner's off?"

"She wants us both to be there." Charisse bit her lip. "Gideon, will you be there?"

"Of course. I'll always be there for you."

Always might possibly end tomorrow. Still she'd left her best friend in tears, and Libby had so few people she could lean upon in times like these. "Gideon, my friend needs me tonight. As much as I'd like to go out to dinner with you, I need to pick up V.J. and come back to the hospital."

"I'll meet you at the school. Can I take Veej for the evening, give you a break, and let you have some time with your friend?"

She closed her eyes and leaned back in her seat. "Why are you always so kind to me, Gideon Tabor?"

"I thought you understood."

Yes, she did. She was one of two women he thought

he might love.

"Would you mind if I invited someone else to join us when we meet with Dee?"

She blinked but swallowed her worries. "Sure."

"Meet me at the school. Veej and I will catch a movie. We'll meet you at home, what, say, nine o'clock?

He always listened to her, remembered everything she said. "You're the most wonderful man in the world, Gideon Tabor." She clicked off the call. "And I'm going to miss you when you tell me good-bye."

Gideon pulled into Charisse's driveway. She'd given him her extra key in case she wasn't home. With the garage door down, he had no way of knowing if she'd arrived before him.

"Veej." He looked into the backseat at the sleeping boy and then got out and opened the door. "Hey, we're home."

"Dad?" V.J. opened his eyes.

A lump in his throat took Gideon's voice away. He would give anything to hear this kid call him by that name. That was a privilege he'd have to earn, and if V.J. didn't want another someone in his life called Dad, Gideon would have to live with it. He cleared his throat. "No, buddy, it's Judge Tabor." He unbuckled the seatbelt and picked up the kid.

V.J. wrapped his arms around Gideon's neck as they moved to the front door. Gideon rang the bell. No answer. He pulled out the key and stuck it in the lock.

He searched for the right switch to light his way up the stairs. Then he toted the boy up the steps and laid him in the bed. V.J. barely roused, but he did reach and pull the covers around him. The kid probably needed to brush his teeth and take a bath, but he was out.

Gideon smiled down at him. They'd done a lot of talking at dinner before the movie. V.J. expected the moon from him, and Gideon hoped he'd be able to deliver. With a little help from Libby and from Charisse's mom, maybe he could take it from the sky and offer it to the boy.

When he'd driven to Titusville the week before and asked Charisse's mother for permission to marry her daughter, the woman could barely contain her happiness. Now, if only Charisse would be that excited.

He moved toward the door.

"Rolf," V.J. called out.

"What, Veej?"

"Where's Rolf?"

His stuffed dog. Gideon looked around the room. Rolf was on the floor tucked between the bed stand and the wall. He picked up the toy and handed it to him. "Night, Veej."

"Night, Dad."

Gideon stared at the boy. V.J.'s eyes were wide open, and his face wore a warm smile. Gideon moved back to him. He sat on the bed. "V.J., I hope God—and your mom—give us the desires of our hearts."

"They will." V.J. hugged Rolf to him. "I know they will, and Mom, she won't punch you either."

"For adults some things are complicated. I've been

too much like a little boy myself. Your mommy may decide I'm not the marrying kind."

"She loves you." V.J. told him.

Gideon placed his hand over V.J.'s heart. "And I love both of you." He leaned forward and kissed the boy's forehead.

"When you marry my mommy, will you have another baby?"

Gideon blinked and his heart beat at a first-time marathon runner's pace. "Would you like that?"

"Yeah."

Gideon smiled and told his heart to slow down. "You're something else, Veej. Let's take this one step at a time. We haven't initiated our plan yet, and it could backfire on me big time."

The garage door rumbled open, and Gideon stood.

"I had a good time tonight," V.J. told him.

"Me, too. Now, go to sleep, or you'll have to brush your teeth and change your clothes. I'll see you tomorrow, okay?"

"Okay." V.J. rolled over and pretended to snore.

Gideon laughed and left the room.

"Gid?" Charisse called from downstairs.

Gideon looked toward the open door to Charisse's room. If he'd been the one who married Charisse first and God called him home, he'd want the next man who loved her to show respect.

Now, though, he imagined what it would be like to be her husband and not to have to go downstairs to greet her. Instead, she'd meet him here at the top of the steps, and they'd walk together to their room where he could hold her against him and show her how much he loved her.

"Honey, I'm home." Charisse's teasing words floated up the stairs.

Gideon moaned and ran down the stairs to greet her.

Chapter Seventeen

Charisse stared at the photograph of Vance still sitting in the frame absent the glass she'd weeks before broken out in her grief.

From the living room entrance, Gideon cleared his throat.

She turned and smiled at the man who'd just arrived. "John." Then she turned a questioning gaze to Gideon. Why did he want his former law partner here with them?

"Whatever Delilah has is apt to be a little subjective," John Turner answered her unspoken inquiry. "Gideon wanted me to come and give you my opinion."

"You think she's still playing games with me?" She directed her question at Gideon.

"Honestly, no," Gideon's friend answered. "One thing about Delilah, she'll toy with you until she doesn't. And if she tells you she's going to be straight with you, she will."

"Why, Mr. Turner, you seem to know a lot about Judge James."

"I probably know more about Delilah than anyone ever should."

Gideon motioned for John to sit.

"What? No comeback?" John raised a brow.

"Not going to kick a friend when he's down, or after I pulled him away from a Magic game."

Charisse looked to him. "Gideon, you had a game tonight, and you asked us to dinner?"

"Tonight? He's been giving me his tickets so much I thought I'd died and gone to basketball heaven." John laughed.

All these nights together with him, she hadn't realized he'd given up his expensive seats.

"V.J. couldn't go on a weekday, and well, I only have two tickets, and the two of us enjoy spending time with you on the weekends."

The doorbell rang, and Gideon moved past her. A muffle of voices came from the foyer.

"I think she's brought someone else with her," Charisse said.

Gideon stepped into the room. He cast a troubled look her way. Delilah entered behind him with another man.

Charisse gasped. "Carson Fullwell."

The man lowered his head. "Mrs. Wellman …"

"I don't understand. Why are you here?" Charisse stepped forward, her eyes narrowed in Delilah's direction. "Why would you bring this man into my house?"

Delilah hurried to her. She leaned close. "Charisse when I spoke with him this afternoon, he asked for an opportunity to speak with you. After I heard his story, I thought you would want to hear what he has to say."

"No." Charisse turned away. "He killed my husband."

Gideon grasped her shoulders. "Charisse, I dismissed the charge against him with my directed verdict."

She pulled from his hold. "You don't think I know

that!"

"I have the file, Charisse. If you want to look at it you can. I'll ask Mr. Fullwell to leave, or you can give him the chance to tell you what the file *doesn't* contain." Delilah held out the manila folder.

"Charisse." John Turner touched her hand. He nodded toward the man who remained in the entrance to her living room. "I haven't seen the file, but I suspect Mr. Fullwell has something important to say to you."

Carson Fullwell wiped his eyes with the back of his hand.

Charisse took a deep breath. She looked about her. Only two worried faces stared back—Delilah and John. Gideon had left the room.

Charisse nodded and straightened. "All right, Mr. Fullwell, I'll give you five minutes."

That was all the grace she had for the man.

Fullwell had aged since she'd last seen him in the halls of the courthouse. He moved like a man condemned.

Charisse closed her eyes and counted to ten. "Please, come in. Have a seat."

"Thank you, Mrs. Wellman." The man took a chair. Delilah sat in the remaining seat, and Charisse sat on the couch beside John Turner. "Gideon?" She looked at John.

"He'll be all right. I suspect the judge wanted you in the hands of better counsel." John winked.

Charisse needed Gideon, and he'd left her alone to face this moment—a moment he'd created. She folded her hands in front of her. "Mr. Fullwell, are you here to tell me you didn't run over and leave my husband to die on the side of the road?"

Carson Fullwell lifted a red-rimmed gaze. "I wish I could tell you that it had been me. If all you wanted was vengeance, I wish I'd entered a guilty plea and not put you through what I'm just beginning to understand has been a nightmare for you."

"Why now? Couldn't you see that I was a grieving wife? What didn't you understand about Vance's son being left behind without a father—a good father—a wonderful father and husband? How could you do this to us? Were you drinking? Did you not understand that you'd left a man dead on the side of the road?" Question after question, buried in her heart for so long, sprang forth. "Mr. Fullwell, I saw your car hit my husband. I saw the aftermath. I can't get it out of my mind. It taints every memory I have of Vance." That memory and the memory of the words of reconciliation she'd never spoken following her angry outburst about the countertop.

The same type of angry words she'd just thrown at Gideon. She'd already broken her promise never to do that to him again.

She started to rise, to find Gideon, to apologize. She never wanted to risk having the same unspoken apology between them and eternity.

"You misunderstand," Mr. Fullwell choked out. "I wasn't driving the car."

The words struck Charisse's heart like an arrow, and she sank back to her seat. "But you know who did? And you hid behind the state's case to help that person go free."

"Yes, ma'am, I did. My court-appointed lawyer said the state didn't have a good case. Of course, I never told him the truth, but when he told me I had a good chance of beating the system, I decided to take it to trial. I wasn't thinking about you or your boy. I was thinking about my son."

Charisse took a deep breath.

Delilah leaned forward. "Charisse, hear the man out."

Charisse jumped to her feet and paced the room.

"I want to tell you how sorry I am," Fullwell started.

Charisse turned, and her gaze fell upon the photograph of her husband.

"I should have done it long ago. When Judge James called me today, I knew God had given me the opportunity I never took." He covered his eyes with his hands. "Six months. That's what they give me. Six months. I need to make everything right with you."

Charisse trembled with fury. "I needed to make apologies to my husband, and I didn't get the chance. The last real conversation I had with him was me screaming at him over a cut on my kitchen counter. I wanted to come home and cook Vance his favorite dinner and tell him how sorry I was for the mean words I'd said to him. He died before I got the chance." She stopped, hands on her hips. Her gaze fell upon her husband's photograph.

Live up to your name, Charisse.

Grace. That's what her name was about. Loving someone when they least deserve it.

Like Christ's love for her.

Her gaze went to Delilah who sat rigid, probably worried she'd done the wrong thing by bringing Carson Fullwell to her home.

Delilah needed an example.

And V.J., who saw her grief and mistook it for anger with his father, didn't need to hear her now.

Vance, Jr., you are to love with all your heart, and if someone breaks your heart, you're to love them twice as hard.

"Oh." Charisse covered her mouth. She turned away from them. She'd shared Vance's words of wisdom with her son, but she'd failed to live them.

"Are you okay?" Delilah was suddenly behind her.

Charisse nodded and gave her attention back to Mr. Fullwell. She took a calm steadying breath. "Mr. Fullwell, I apologize to you." She closed her eyes and again breathed in deeply. With her hands on her thighs, she lowered to the couch. "I'm ready to listen." She stood again. "Before you go on, may I offer you a bottled water, some iced tea?"

The man shook his head and again wiped his eyes. "Thank you, but I'm fine."

Again, Charisse sank to the couch and waited.

"My son," Mr. Fullwell began but held up his hand. He took a moment to recover his emotions and then nodded as if to convince himself he could do it. "Thomas, my boy, he's the one who hit your husband, Mrs. Wellman. He wasn't drinking. He was just nineteen. He—he said a car moved into his lane. The way he told it to me, he swerved to avoid the collision. His attention was on that. He didn't check to see that the shoulder was clear. He didn't see your husband in time."

Charisse swallowed. Just like Gideon's accident. Only Gideon was a grown man with driving skills most nineteen-year-old boys wouldn't have. She focused her gaze on the smiling face of her husband even though she couldn't see it through the tears clouding her vision. If it had been her who died on the side of the road, Vance would have forgiven Mr. Fullwell before the trial.

"Thomas panicked. He sped away, and he drove home."

Charisse nodded, and the tears fell down her face like a flowing river. Still, she focused on Vance.

"He wanted to turn himself in, but me—I'm the one who refused to let him do it. You see, he was shipping out to Afghanistan the next day. We weren't a rich family. It was his opportunity to join the military so that he could attend college when he returned. He wanted to be an engineer. I couldn't let him throw it all away."

John cleared his throat. "You waited for the police to figure it out, and when they traced the tag, you let them think you were responsible."

Charisse didn't break contact with Vance's smile.

"By that time, Thomas had deployed." Mr. Fullwell stood blocking Charisse's vision of the photograph.

"Would you have gone to prison for him?" she asked. "Would he allow you to do that?"

Mr. Fullwell bowed his head. "He would have done whatever I told him to do. He was a good boy like that. But if you're asking me if he had a conscience, yes, ma'am, he did. And he wrote me time after time, asking me for permission to tell the truth."

A thousand questions crossed her mind as Mr. Fullwell dug into his wallet. He pulled out a photograph and lifted it toward Charisse.

She reached and took it in her trembling fingers.

A handsome serious-faced teen dressed in combat fatigues with a black beret covering most of his short-cropped blond hair looked back at her. She studied the solemn face.

"Mrs. Wellman, he had his life before him. I wanted him to have a future."

Charisse handed the photo back to the young man's father.

"In today's world, there's a tendency of the media to paint anyone who makes a mistake in a bad light. They wouldn't understand that my boy had a kind heart. That he was an Eagle Scout, and he volunteered to work with the elderly. They wouldn't know he'd helped me care for his mother who died when he was sixteen. The press would paint him as a coldhearted teenager who left your husband on the side of the road." He slipped back into the chair. "He always did what I asked. Always. Never gave me a bit of trouble."

Charisse looked at the picture again. "Now that you've told me, will you allow him to confess?

"Charisse …" Delilah remained close. She touched Charisse's arm.

Charisse shrugged from her. "Mr. Fullwell, will you allow Thomas to come back to stand before a court of law?"

Mr. Fullwell looked from Delilah and back to her. "We—I've already been judged, Mrs. Wellman."

She blinked. "I don't understand."

"Thomas was killed in Afghanistan." The man broke down. "My only son, my only family gone. I'm all alone."

John hurried to his side, pulling out a handkerchief.

Mr. Fullwell waved it off and pulled out his own. "Mrs. Wellman, Thomas died but not before he saved five members of his battalion. As far as I know, they're still alive today because Thomas pulled them out of danger. He took a bullet going in to check for others."

Charisse bowed her head. The tears fell one after the other without any other outward sign of her anguish. Silent grief.

She didn't dare look up at the man sitting across the room or at the picture of her husband she'd focused upon.

Vance wouldn't want her to carry this pain. He certainly would never want her to make this dying man suffer any more than he had already.

I'm sorry for yelling at you that day, Vance. I'm so sorry. She squeezed her eyes closed even tighter and took deep breaths to settle her soul. She may not have been able to apologize to Vance, but she could make up for it, put this behind her and behind Mr. Fullwell.

She opened her eyes and wiped at her moist cheeks. She pressed upward to her feet and took shaky steps to the bookshelf. She took down Vance's photograph, lifting it from the glassless frame. Then she sank to her knees in front of the man who still sat with his head down, choking sobs falling from his broken spirit. "Mr. Fullwell." She placed a hand over his. "Please forgive me."

He jerked his gaze to hers. "I don't understand."

"Forgive me for making you feel unwelcome in my home, for letting you believe I would never forgive you or your son." She squeezed his hand and held up Vance's photo. "My husband was a better man than I've shown him to be. He offered forgiveness readily. So I hope you will forgive me for taking so long to forgive you."

"Thomas, he was just a boy who made a terrible mistake. Me—I made the wrong decisions for both of us. If I'd allowed him to turn himself in like he wanted, he'd be alive today."

Charisse shook her head. "Don't you see?"

"See what, ma'am?"

"Five men lived that day in Afghanistan because you did what you did. If Thomas hadn't been there to save them, quite possibly all five of them would have died. Thomas had nothing to prove, but in doing what he did, I can see he was raised well. He paid the ultimate sacrifice, giving his life in exchange for those others. My husband wasn't doing anything as heroic, but he stopped to help an elderly man with his car. Don't hold my actions against Vance. He taught me about forgiveness as well as you must have taught your son about sacrifice."

Charisse touched the photo of Thomas Fullwell that his father held in his hand. "May I keep this?"

Mr. Fullwell nodded.

"Thank you." She stood and held out her hand. "And Mr. Fullwell, you are not alone."

The man got shakily to his feet.

"You have me and you have my son. The families of Vance Wellman and Thomas Fullwell will prove that neither died in vain."

John Turner hugged her, and Delilah touched her shoulders as they stood out on her porch. Mr. Fullwell stopped. "Thank you, Mrs. Wellman."

"Charisse." She smiled. "I have your number, and V.J. and I will be bringing over some meals for you next week."

He nodded. "I look forward to meeting your boy. Good night."

Charisse smiled. "Good night." She waited for them to leave before closing and locking the door. She needed to call Gideon, to apologize to him for her outburst.

She'd made his decision easy for him. *Run to the other woman as fast as you can.*

"Charisse?" Gideon stepped out of the kitchen.

She put her hand to her heart. "I thought you left. I was about to call you to apologize."

"Apologize?"

"Gideon, I already failed in my promise to you, but I know now. God gave me a very real reminder of why forgiveness is so important."

"I heard. I saw." His gaze softened. "Vance Wellman was a good man. So much better than this one."

"Vance was a different man, but Gideon since my father left me, I've always looked for integrity in the men I love."

He narrowed his eyes. "How many have there been?" A smile slid his lips into an upward curve.

She slapped him. "Three."

"Three?" He leaned away from her.

"That idiot from high school ..."

"An idiot with integrity, now that's something you don't hear about every day?"

"Like I was saying, that idiot in high school, Vance,

and you."

"Well, maybe you'll get a chance to practice your forgiveness on the idiot tomorrow night."

"He's forgiven. Honestly and truly."

Gideon looked at his watch. "Well, if I'm going to meet up with my old friend tomorrow night so we can all set a course for our lives, I need to go home and get my beauty sleep." He didn't move, and Charisse wondered if he would kiss her, and if he kissed her would it make his curiosity over the other woman disappear.

"'Night, Charisse. I guess I won't get a chance to see you tomorrow until we meet up at the reunion."

She nodded. "'Night, Gideon. Thank you for taking V.J. tonight. You probably don't remember her, but Libby Overstreet's mother is in the hospital, and she needed someone."

"You're still friends with Libby?"

"She's my best friend, has been since before high school." Charisse tilted her head. What was that look all about—a half smile, a twinkle in his green eyes.

"I didn't know you two were still friends. Really?" He darted his gaze everywhere but at her.

"Gid?"

He shook his head and moved toward the door.

"Gideon Tabor?"

"'Night, Charisse."

"Is it Libby? You had a crush on Libby Overstreet?"

He paused and looked to the ceiling. "Tomorrow night is going to be very interesting." He opened the door and slipped through it before she could reach him.

"Libby ..." she breathed her friend's name. "Now

that I know it's you, how could I ever ask you to give up a man like Gideon Tabor?" She locked the door and with her back to it, slid down the wall. "God, Libby deserves a man like Gideon. Don't let me stand in the way of my friend's happiness no matter how much it hurts."

She widened her eyes as the truth dawned.

"That's why he wanted me to tutor him. He needed an excuse to get close to Libby."

FAY LAMB

Chapter Eighteen

Charisse stood in the back of the room watching Libby converse with several of their fellow classmates.

They'd been together most of the day, and every time Charisse mentioned Gideon to Libby, her friend's cheeks blazed red, and she couldn't hold Charisse's gaze. How could she have been so blind not to see Libby had feelings for the big oaf? Libby had listened to her cry, had even joked with her, made her laugh in the midst of her tears, and all the while, she loved Gideon, too.

She would not let this harm their friendship. Libby was Gideon's first love, and she was such a sweet woman.

Then why did the thought of Libby in Gideon's arms cause Charisse's heart to ache.

Libby left the conversation and came to stand beside Charisse. "Are you okay? You've been pretty quiet today?"

Charisse sighed as she placed her arm loosely around Libby's shoulder. "Two months ago, I didn't believe the five of us would pull this together."

"We did a good job, didn't we?"

As the banquet room began to fill with classmates, Charisse sensed anticipation building. Each time the door opened, she and every other person seemed to hold their breath waiting for the arrival of the class's white knight. Several women, who served as Gideon's constant shadow

FAY LAMB

during high school, mentioned his name as they passed, and if Charisse didn't know better, she thought they looked at her in an odd way.

"Are you as nervous as I am?" Libby remained close to Charisse.

"Why? Should I be?" Charisse moved to the punch table. She gripped the plastic cup and fought the trembling in her hand as she raised the ladle.

"Gideon will be here."

"He's wonderful, isn't he?" Charisse lifted the cup to her lips. "Libby, there's something you should know."

"I think it's romantic. You've worked with him all this time, and tonight there's going to be a lot of surprises. He's coming here to see the woman he used to love, and Charisse, he's going to choose you."

"No, Libby. He's going to choose the other woman."

Libby reached for her own glass and the ladle. She poured the pink punch and put the glass to her lips.

Charisse lifted her smile in what she hoped looked like a confident air. "Because you're the other woman?"

Libby choked then gasped.

"And Libby, I'm so happy about it, because we're best friends, and V.J. won't lose his overgrown friend."

"What are you talking about?" Libby's voice reached an octave Charisse never believed humanly possible.

People turned and stared, and Libby pulled her back away from the crowd.

"It's you he's coming to see, and Libby he is so wonderful and kind."

"Yes, he is wonderful and sweet, but there's only one problem."

"You'll be so happy." Charisse tried to fight the quiver of her lips, but her courage failed her. "Did you ever imagine that you were the one?"

"Never in a thousand years." Libby rolled her eyes upward. "Listen to you acting like you could walk away from that man and let him go to another woman."

"Not just any woman." Tears spilled over her eyes. "You ... and ... I'm ... so ... happy ... for ... you."

Libby smiled. "You love him so much, you'd make such a sacrifice? You won't even fight me for him?"

"I love you that much." Charisse sniffled.

"Well, here's the thing—"

The door opened and a hush fell over the room.

The crowd was in as much awe of him as V.J.'s second-grade class. Did Gideon realize the command he had of this adoring throng? Her heart stopped as she watched the benevolent knight surrounded by his serfs. He was handsome in a white button-down shirt, sleeves rolled upward with care, and hunter green slacks. A strand of brown hair fell across his forehead in a careless manner, making his boyish smile even more charming. She heard his familiar deep laugh as he listened to the chatter around him, but he seemed preoccupied, looking around for someone.

He was looking for the love of his life, and she stood right beside her. Libby. Not her. Charisse's heart dove into a deep pit of despair. She didn't want a single moment with Gideon. She desired a lifetime.

"Charisse." Libby backed into her. "He sees you."

"You. He sees you." Charisse moved around behind her.

Across the room, Gideon's green-eyed gaze met hers, and he smiled.

Gideon looked around the Royal Oak Country Club banquet room. The committee had done a wonderful job with the decorations.

He spied Charisse in the center of the room. She and Libby began a funny little dance, circling around behind each other. A smile crossed his face. He'd been in love with the same beautiful woman twice in one lifetime.

Charisse stepped behind Libby, and Libby glared in his direction. "Really?" She mouthed, scrunching up her nose and hitting her hand to her forehead.

He bit his lip and made a face. Yeah, maybe his last minute red herring hadn't been that great of an idea.

Libby made a quick motion with her hand, imploring him to come to the rescue.

He gave a slow shake of his head, and Libby stomped her foot at him as Charisse ducked further back into the room.

Still, he kept Charisse in his sights. How could he think of anything with her beauty outshining everyone else in the room? She had bound her blonde locks into a bun, with soft tendrils falling down. She wore just a touch of makeup, enough to make her cheeks glow. A blue sweater top and a matching print skirt draped her slender figure. Already, he could see many of their classmates wondered at the Cinderella standing in their midst. He was no Prince Charming, but he would love Fair Charisse all the days of his life—if she'd only let him. *God, please, let me love her the way You intend for a man to love a woman, completely and passionately.*

Charisse turned from him as Libby shook her head and followed, bumping into his princess who braced herself against a potential fall. They both managed to stay on their feet. Gideon started in their direction.

"We hear you're a judge now, Gid, and Charisse is working for you."

Gideon turned his attention to the woman who addressed him. Her nametag said she was Debbie York. He didn't remember her.

"Some lucky man is going to find a wonderful bride, isn't he?" she asked and nodded in Charisse's direction.

"I don't know." But by the grace of God, he would soon—and he'd not only be a husband. He'd be a father to a little boy he loved dearly. He looked again in Charisse's direction, but both she and Libby had disappeared.

He searched the room. A large crowd gathered at a table in the corner. He wandered over. "What's going on?" he asked Roger Wright.

"You don't want to know. Women." Roger pulled him away. "So, how's life treating you, Gideon?"

Gideon leaned back and looked out into the foyer. He'd left something precious there, and he wanted to make sure the hands he'd entrusted his treasure to were keeping it safe.

Everyone mingled, and an occasional burst of

laughter rang out in the crowd, always in the general vicinity of Gideon. "Why doesn't he get this over with? He's been waiting to see you for forever," Charisse mumbled. "And you're hiding over here in the corner with me. Libby get out there so he can find you."

"Charisse, do you really think he's here for me?"

"He told me."

Libby shook her head. "He's a dead man."

Charisse stared at her. Libby never spoke like that about anyone.

"I'd like to show you something." Libby started away but stopped when Charisse didn't follow. "Come on, silly." Libby took her hand and pulled Charisse with her until they stood in front of the Wall of Memories. Libby pointed to a picture Charisse had never viewed.

"Where did you find this?" She touched the glossy color photo.

"I found it when Karen and I went through the yearbook photos Dick Majors gave us, but I didn't need this picture to see what I already knew even in high school."

"Gideon's every bit as handsome now as he was then."

Libby made Charisse step back for a better observation. "Don't you see it, Charisse?"

"What?"

Libby cupped her hand over Charisse's image to allow her to look solely at Gideon's face. "What do you see in his eyes?"

"Amusement. I was a funny looking creature."

Charisse

"Charisse." Libby nodded toward the picture. "Look at the love showing in his face." She lowered her hand. "And you're looking at him the same way."

In the picture, Gideon stood facing her in front of the school. He smiled down at her, and she looked up at him. Charisse stared at his handsome face, wanting more than anything to believe Libby's romantic notion—but the romance belonged to her best friend. "Libby, he loved you. I was so—"

"Besides being gullible, you were and are the most beautiful woman I have ever known, Charisse Taylor Wellman."

Charisse's heart leapt into her throat at the sound of his voice. She turned and looked into his deep green eyes. "What?"

"You, Charisse. You're the woman I came here tonight to see."

Her heart lifted like a hot air balloon rising to the heavens. Then it fell to the earth. "Why you, pompous, no good, scallywag. I ought to never speak with you again. How could you make me think all these weeks that you were in love with another woman?"

"Because I was. I loved Charisse Taylor, and now I love the woman she's become. I love you Charisse Wellman."

"Gideon Tabor, you—you big oaf." She stomped away from him.

"What about that promise you made to me." He reached for her hand.

"What?" She rounded on him then blinked. "Null and void, buster. You made me think it was Libby? All day,

I've wondered how I could give you up to my best friend."

"Libby." Gideon nodded his hello. "How have you been? Good to see you."

"I'm—I'm fine. How are you?"

"I'm doing well. Would you excuse my soon-to-be ex-law clerk for a moment?"

"His ex-law clerk?" Whispers buzzed around them.

He again took Charisse by the arm.

"Let me go," she repeated. "I'm not your soon-to-be anything! I quit!" She started in the other direction.

"Charisse."

She kept moving.

"Charisse, you can't quit because you're fired!"

The watching crowd collectively gasped.

Fury made her world spin. The monster-clone had made a triumphant return. Refuse him, and he threw a temper tantrum. But how could she explain this abandonment to V.J.?

"Did you hear me?" he baited.

She spun toward him. "I'm fired? You have the nerve to fire me after all you've put me through?"

"Yeah, you're fired."

A symphony of "uh-ohs" broke forth in the room.

"Because my wife can't work for me."

"You'll break V.J.'s heart. He loves you as much as I do."

"Charisse." From somewhere nearby, Libby warned. "Listen to him."

"And I want my wife to finish law school so we can someday practice together while we raise a houseful of children."

"You are the most exasperating, vile, irritating man."

"I kind of like your place. After the wedding, I'd like to live there. I don't want V.J. to feel displaced. It can be hard on a kid. By the way, I'm bringing my dog into the marriage. That okay?"

"Spoiled, never satisfied."

Houseful of children.

Wedding.

Marriage.

Cletus ... that wonderful big, goofy dog.

She swallowed hard. "Did you say wedding?"

Eyebrows raised, he nodded.

"Did you say wife?"

Again he nodded, his lips curving into a smile.

Around them, the crowd remained hushed.

The rest of his words sunk in. Tears sprang to her eyes. "Gid." She breathed out his name. "A houseful of kids?"

"I can stand five or six more. You?"

"I thought you wanted nine or ten?"

"I didn't want to push my luck and make you run the other way. Let's start with the one I need to adopt first. He wants to call me Dad. I think Judge Tabor is a little too formal now, don't you?"

"V.J.? You've talked this over with my son?"

"I'd like to make him mine. He asked me first."

"What?" She laughed.

"I told you he's a master at the setup. You didn't believe me. He planned this entire scenario."

"Yeah, I bet." Behind her, Libby snorted. "I guess it

was V.J.'s idea to let Charisse think I was the love of your life?"

"No, actually that idea came to me at the last minute. I'm thinking, not my brightest moment."

"Ya think?" Libby shook her head.

Gideon turned his amused smile from Libby to Charisse. "Well, what's your answer?"

Charisse's heart soared into the heavens. She'd been conniving, working, and barely surviving. While she'd tried to get by on her own devices, holding on to her grief and her anger, God had worked His own plan. He'd given her provision and he'd shown her the freedom of forgiveness and both bloomed into a beautiful promise, a promise of a husband, and of a loving father for her son.

A promise I broke again.

Gideon turned toward the door and nodded at Karen who motioned someone inside.

V.J. ran toward them. Gideon swooped him up into his arms. "Your mother let me borrow him. Leverage." He raised his brows.

V.J. had known the best of a father's love, and God had seen fit to allow him to have the heart of another wise earthly father. One who forgave her as readily as his natural father had always done.

"Charisse?" Gideon asked.

"Mommy, say yes," V.J. begged.

She couldn't speak. Instead, she shook her head in disbelief. God had proven Himself faithful despite her faithlessness and her bitterness.

"No?" The precious smile left Gideon's face, and V.J.'s lips started to tremble.

"No?" The hushed word reverberated through the crowd.

Gideon lowered his head, the little boy pout matching the one on her son's face spoke volumes to her.

"Gideon, what kind of fool would I be if I told God I didn't want the wonderful gift he'd prepared for me and for my son? I'm sorry for being angry with you—again."

"Yes?" He seemed unsure, so unlike the commanding figure who entered the room at the beginning of the evening.

"There would be no living with my son if I didn't say yes."

V.J. brought his elbow into his side, fist clenched, palm up—Gideon's victory sign.

"Charisse, please answer me?" Gideon put her son down and knelt on one knee before her.

Had his lips quivered, too? Did he not hear the same words that caused her son's reaction? He loved her that much? She stared down into those compassionate green eyes. "Yes, Gideon. Yes." She reached for his hands and pulled him to his feet. "I will marry you, and God willing, we'll have as many children as you want."

He reached for her and pulled her close. "At this moment, all that matters to me is you and V.J. and taking care of what God has given me."

He tilted his head then leaned toward her. His lips brushed against hers.

She leaned into him, not willing to let him go.

"I love you so much." He kissed her again with a passion that made her ache for the years of tenderness his caress promised.

"Ahem." Roger stood beside them. He held a gigantic card made from poster board. The front of the card held a larger copy of the picture Libby had shown Charisse on the Wall of Memories. "Those women I told you about earlier. Libby had them scheming behind your backs. Everyone here wants you to know we're so happy the two of you finally figured out what we knew in high school. You were made for each other. Gideon, Charisse we want to give you your first wedding gift—a Caribbean cruise."

Charisse turned to her friend. Libby took a step backward. Charisse pointed her finger and laughed. "You are a little rat. I'm offering him to you on a silver platter, and you knew about his plan the entire time."

"No, now, Gideon, you tell her. I got into this plan late in the game."

Gideon slipped his arm around Charisse's waist. "What our wonderful friend is trying to tell you is I enlisted her on my side." He narrowed his eyes at Libby. "And she got the best of both of us."

"Libby Overstreet." Charisse laughed. "You just wait. One day, I'm going to get back at you."

Libby threw her arms around her. "I hope you do. I really hope you do."

Gideon kissed the top of Charisse's hair. "Now you know, Charisse Taylor Wellman. My heart has always been yours."

Charisse turned in his arms. She started to speak, but he placed a finger to her lips.

"I thank God for Vance Wellman." He looked down at the little boy by their side. "God knew that someday

Vance's son would need another man to act in his place. I'm glad I'm the one He chose."

Chapter Nineteen

Charisse looked in the mirror at the beautiful gown of satin and lace. She ran her hands over the pearl inlays and looked at the other two women dressed in yellow and standing behind her.

"Momma and I wanted you to loan you this." Libby handed Charisse a small white Bible. "She thought it would be nice for you to carry down the aisle."

Charisse opened the tiny book and leafed through the pages. "Something borrowed," she whispered.

"Something blue." Delilah handed her a blue ribbon. Charisse opened the Bible to Proverbs 31. Delilah looked up at her. "Perfect." She slipped the ribbon in the crease. Charisse closed it.

"Sorry we don't have anything new," Libby said.

"Or old," Delilah added.

Charisse smiled at her friends. "The borrowed and the blue are fine."

A knock at the door caused them to spin around. "Are you gals decent?" Deacon asked.

Libby opened the door. "We are, and we're ready."

Delilah pressed a bouquet of yellow roses, absent the thorns, into her hand, and the thought that the old Delilah would have replaced the florist's bouquet with thorny stems brought a smile to Charisse.

"They say yellow roses denote that a man only wants

to be friends," Delilah said. "But I think they are so appropriate for you and Gideon. He's the kind of man who can be your husband and your best friend at the same time." Delilah smirked. "God bless you, Charisse. You two goofs are perfect for one another."

Charisse hugged Delilah to her. "He won't ever admit it, but he loves you, Dee. He torments you because you're like a sister to him."

Delilah gave a brief squeeze and released her. "Make him happy." She followed Libby out the door and down the stairs.

Charisse got to the threshold and turned. She glanced at the place where Vance's picture once sat. She'd put it away, ready to start a new life, but sadness lingered, mixing with the euphoric thought of becoming Gideon's bride.

She'd traded the wedding photo for the engagement photo Gideon had insisted he wanted to use for their wedding announcement: Charisse sat at in the backyard swing in a white sundress, her hands grasping the swing's ropes. Gideon stood behind her, his hands covering hers.

From this day forward this room would belong to her and to Gideon. He'd never stepped inside of it, always standing at the door, never entering—her gentlemanly hero.

"Darlin'." Deacon moved beside her. "You okay?"

Charisse turned to him. She bit her lip and nodded. "I'm the luckiest woman in the world. God has graced me with the love of two wonderful men." She looked down. "I'm having trouble letting go of one to hold on to the other."

"Ah, darlin', you don't have to let go. Let the love Vance showed you shine through to Gideon."

Charisse nodded, and linking her arm in his, she strolled down the stairs.

Libby and Delilah waited on her back porch. When Charisse came into view, they opened the screen door and stepped out to join Gideon's groomsmen.

As Gideon had described the day he'd gotten all their friends to landscape her yard—soon to be theirs—Marlene had done a wonderful job decorating the lawn for the wedding. Chairs with yellow covers lined each side of the path. Yellow roses skirted an area in front of the garden.

Charisse's pastor stood in the garden, surrounded by white azaleas. To his left were the two most handsome men in the world—Gideon and V.J., dressed in black tuxes with light yellow cummerbunds.

A violinist from Deacon's church began to play the wedding march, and Deacon pushed open the door for her. They stood for a second, and Charisse caught her breath.

Frozen for a moment, she didn't move.

"Charisse?" Deacon whispered.

Charisse looked up and stared across the yard. She tightened her hold on the bouquet and Bible and steadied her gaze on Gideon's face. He smiled, and she looked to Deacon. "I'm ready."

Deacon tucked her hand into the crook of his arm and covered it with his hand. "I'm real proud of the boy," he said. "Think of him like a son. His father left behind a fine young man."

Charisse nodded and pressed her nose against the bouquet, drinking in the sweet aroma of the roses. "Yes, he did."

She took the first step and the second, and with each one she began to let go of Vance and move toward her new life with the man waiting for her at the altar.

Gideon never flinched when she or V.J. shared stories about Vance. He listened with interest. He allowed her and V.J. to cry and to laugh. In quiet times alone, he encouraged her to share her thoughts with him. He never rebuked her for not letting go of the *other* man.

As they reached the end of the aisle, Charisse handed the bouquet to Libby.

"Who gives this woman to this man in marriage?" the pastor asked.

Deacon stepped away from her, drawing something from his pocket. The gold chain and a ring—her wedding ring from Vance—shined in the sunlight.

Charisse brought her trembling hand to her heart. Gideon didn't want her or her son to forget about the past they'd shared with Vance. Gideon expected it to complete them—to add to their marriage and his father-son relationship with V.J.

How many times had Gideon said he respected Vance? At the park that day when V.J.'s grief finally broke, spilling out in sobs, he spoke about the chain and the ring and what they would mean to him. Those weren't vain words. "Oh," she whispered as the tears fell. She wiped them away.

"On behalf of Vance Wellman, Sr., and Vance Wellman, Jr., I do." Deacon opened the clasp of the chain and waited for Charisse to turn. He slipped it around her neck and closed the clasp.

She hugged Deacon close to her. "Something old and something new."

"He loves you, Darlin'." Deacon backed away.

Gideon shook Deacon's hand then took his place beside her, his little-boy grin lighting up his face. He reached out and took both of her hands in his. "Charisse," he leaned toward her. "I'm so glad you wore white."

Discussion Questions

1. Charisse's name means, *grace, beauty, kindness.*
Though Charisse couldn't see that she still maintained
those attributes after her husband's death, in what way are
they shown to Gideon?

2. When he was a teenager, Gideon's father died in what
seemed a sudden loss for Gideon. Charisse tried to help
him through his grief by introducing him to Christ.
Gideon acted out of his grief and in so doing, he hurt
Charisse. What positive impact on others in the story did
Gideon's past behavior have when he finally understood
the gift Charisse tried to share with him?

3. Judge Deacon Foster continually tries to tell Gideon
that he needs to stay away from the brash Judge Delilah
James. Gideon continues, though, to attempt to be friends
with Delilah. In your opinion, should Gideon have
distanced himself away from the woman who seemed to
want more than friendship, or should he have heeded
Deacon's advice?

4. Despite Charisse's efforts to distance herself from
Gideon, to remain angry with him, she is drawn closer to
him for several reason, the most compelling is the fact
that her son, V.J. seems to slowly emerge from his grief.
At the same time, Charisse fails to see her own
emergence. How does Gideon pull both mother and son
from their lethargy and pain?

5. When Delilah tells Charisse about her new relationship with Christ, Charisse is skeptical, but even though Delilah does very little out of character, what do you suppose was the overall fact that made Charisse realize that Delilah told the truth? Do you believe that Charisse would have believed Delilah's announcement if Delilah's personality had instantly changed? Why or why not?

6. Gideon never went beyond the threshold of Charisse's bedroom door, even when he carried her up the stairs. Why do you think this was important to him or why do you believe he refrained from entering her room? What importance did it hold to Charisse on her wedding day?

About the Author

Fay Lamb offers services as a freelance editor, and is an author of Christian romance and romantic suspense. Her emotionally charged stories remind the reader that God is always in the details.

Fay has served as secretary for American Christian Fiction Writer's operating board and as a moderator for ACFW's critique group, Scribes. For her volunteer efforts for ACFW, she received the Service Members Award in 2010.

Fay and her husband, Marc, reside in Titusville, Florida, where multi-generations of their families have lived. The legacy continues with their two married sons and five grandchildren.

Visit Fay on the Web:
www.FayLamb.com

Charisse is the first in a four-book series, so watch for these stories in the coming months: *Liberty*, *Hope*, and *Delilah*.

More Books by Fay Lamb

Stalking Willow

Bitterness, a stalker, and a neighbor to die for. What's a girl to do? Trailed by a stalker in New York City, Willow Thomas, a young ad executive, scurries back to her small North Carolina hometown and the lake house where ten years earlier a scandal revealed her entire life had been a lie, and a seed of bitterness took root in her soul. The cocoon of safety Willow feels upon her arrival home soon unravels when she meets opposition from her family, faces the man she left behind, and the stalker reveals he is close on her heels. Can Willow learn to trust God to tear out her roots of resentment, reunite her family, ferret out a deadly stalker, and to rekindle the love she left behind?

Available on Amazon, Kindle, Barnes & Noble, and by order from your favorite bookseller.

Better Than Revenge (Coming Later This Year)

Michael's fiancée, Issie Putnam, was brutally attacked and Michael was imprisoned for a crime he didn't commit. Now he's home to set things right.

Two people stand in his way: Issie's son, Cole, and a madman.

Can Michael learn to love the child Issie holds so close to her heart and protect him from the man who took everything from Michael so long ago?

Look for other books

published by

Pix-N-Pens Publishing

www.PixNPens.com

and

www.WriteIntegrity.com

Made in United States
Orlando, FL
31 March 2025